OTLEY FOREVER

OTLEY FOREVER

by

MARTIN WADDELL

𝔰𝔡

STEIN AND DAY/*Publishers*/New York

Stein and Day/*Publishers*/7 East 48 Street, New York, N.Y. 10017

CHAPTER ONE

'Shop?' I said, very softly, and waited, making a rapid survey of the stock. Then a minstrel boy followed a fat little Chinaman into my coat pocket, without so much as a second's fumble.

My market bag is only human, more's the pity, so I couldn't take the lot. Two pieces of soapstone went into my bag, and a Mosaic brooch for Imogen, small pieces that might never be missed. There remained some nice stuff, but taking it all would have been immoral, though it was robbing the rich. Decisions were called for, backed by the taste and discrimination that puts a man in the Portobello bracket. Not for the first time I regretted leaving my shoplifter's coat in London when I might have known I would need it.

Expensive snuffboxes, I thought, miniature tea-sets, lovely.

Then I caught sight of the management. He was eyeing me from his position on the floor, his view obscured by the top of a magnificent pie-crust table, and he didn't so much as howl in protest at the gaps in his stock.

'Mr. Garvey?' I said, trying to sound respectable but absent minded, the sort of person who drops pretty things in market bags without meaning to.

5

He didn't answer me, which wasn't unreasonable, as he was dead.

He lay quite still, gazing at me past the ice-pick which protruded from his chest. His blood-stained shirt had once been white and his tie Old Etonian, to which he was not entitled. He looked every inch an Englishman, though I knew for a fact that he carried Wog credentials, for his real name was Lebnowitz and he was the distant cousin of a Russian count. His benign smile didn't fool me a bit, I knew he'd been basically nasty.

Courage, I thought, then dynamic action.

So I put my market bag in a place of safety and went through to the back parlour of Anastasia Antiques to telephone M.2. It took me some time to get through, because the peasant on the Dublin Telephone Exchange had not mastered the rudiments of the English language.

'Hullo Alice,' I said to Alice Alexander, the powerhouse of the organisation, a chip off the old Empire. 'This is Gerald Otley speaking.' She said something which I thought uncalled for, but it was no time for badinage. 'Listen carefully,' I said, interrupting her. 'I have seen the man you sent me to. He is unable to talk ... unable to. Do you understand?'

'Yes,' she said. I'll say one thing for Bandy Alice, she is quick on the uptake, but then she has to be, because she more or less runs M.2 on her tod.

'Good,' I said, trying to convey how deeply good it was of her down the line. Normally our relations are not of the best, but I had to own myself absolutely pro-Alice this time.

'I am with Anastasia,' I said, phrasing it with in-

finite care for the benefit of any Fenian wiretapper
who might be at work. 'What do you want me to
do?'

'You must persuade Garvey to take his leave of us,'
she said. 'Tell him he must go.'

'Where?' I said.

'For a swim,' she said.

'No,' I said, appalled.

'Yes,' she said. 'It is most important. Afterwards
you must keep Anastasia company and await our
further instructions. Is that understood? We shall be
getting in touch with you as soon as we hear from
Father.'

'Listen,' I said. 'Why can't I just ring up the Gardai
and...' But the line had gone dead. She was all right
sipping tea in London with her secret service friends,
she hadn't got a corpulent middle-European corpse
on her hands, making a mess all over the lino. Just
the same I was thrilled at my name getting through to
Father circles, where He might see it. Basically, I'm
for England, Harold, and the other George.

Back into the shop I went. Garvey had not moved,
which was a pleasant surprise. In this business corpses
have a habit of disappearing when you turn your back
on them. Then I remembered that I was organising
the disappearing, and the moment lost its charm.

It was just past midnight, with no moon to light
the streets of Dublin. Great. I took swim as a euphem-
ism for sink, which seemed to me an example of
pretty slick thinking from Alice's end, bearing in
mind that Anastasia Antiques was down on the
Dublin Quays, with the Liffey slipping past the front
door. All I had to do was to carry Garvey across the

road and drop him in, then sit in Anastasia's waiting for further instructions whilst my name echoed down the corridors of power.

If he was to go to the bottom of the Liffey and stay there he would need to be well weighed down, so I started sorting through his tat for heavy things to put in his pockets. I selected an iron sheepdog and two tins of nails, then added all the coal I could find in his scuttle. It didn't add up to concrete feet, but I felt I'd done my bit.

I looked up and down the quay cautiously, then propped the door open with an old riding boot. A short sprint to the river wall would do it. Garvey might well have picked his shop with corpse disposal in mind, I thought, lightheartedly, then I realised there was no might about it.

But the corpse was there and so was I, and Britain, in the person of Bandy Alice of M.2, had called. Apart from the patriotic angle I expected to get well paid for it, being on the M.2 staff on a now-and-then basis. Alice doesn't approve of me because of my irregular methods and my friend Grace, who is a tough lady and not to be trusted unless she fancies you. If Grace fancies you you're probably all right and if she doesn't you're probably not. J don't know who she works for but she seems to be for Elizabeth and Empire and all that I hold dear, in her own peculiar way, and she is nice. I looked at dead Garvey and thought what a pity it was that Grace wasn't around to advise me, having good reason to believe her a dab hand at corpse disposal, an empirical art.

'Easy,' I said, to Pope Paul who happened to be watching me at the time from the rear of the oil heater. It was all a question of confidence. No trouble, I thought.

Grab Garvey, dash out, splash, dash back in again.

So I grabbed Garvey. Garvey was very heavy. That was as far as I got, dashing was out of the question.

There was a little green van in the yard at the back of Anastasia Antiques which seemed ideally suited to my foul purpose. I removed the bags of cement from the back but I left the sten gun where it was, thinking that it might come in handy sometime. Then I went back to the shop for Garvey, unloaded the coal and the iron sheepdog from his pockets, and dragged him by the shoulders through the back parlour and out into the yard, nearly doing myself an injury on his electric kettle in the process.

I hoisted him into the back of the van and got into the front myself, to rest. He was much too fat and flabby for a top-flight agent, there had certainly been nothing brutal and sexy about him. I had a vague idea that Dublin might be where they put the old boys out to grass after the fun and fury of Berlin with all those nasty triple crossings. Dublin belonged to my aesthetic-self, the pad of Oscar and James and Sean and William Butler and the Abbey and Shamrock Rovers. People don't get slaughtered with icepicks in that sort of place, or at least they don't in my book.

It was unfortunate that at that moment I bethought myself of the market bag I was leaving behind me, and decided to go back and collect it, just to be on the safe side. If I hadn't gone back I wouldn't have been standing in the parlour when someone shuffled through the front door.

Trouble. So I put down the Wedgwood piece I'd been inspecting, which was the wrong colour anyway, and darted up the stairs past Garvey's Egyptian drapes, wishing I'd thought to bring the sten gun with me.

I expected a few minutes pause and then a shrill harsh scream from the backyard and the sound of the newcomer summoning the Gardai, but nothing of the sort happened. Instead I heard a lot of muttering down below, what seemed like a worried conversation. From the banging and bumping that followed I gathered somebody was searching for something.

It didn't take a masterbrain to work out what that would be. Dead Garvey. It also seemed reasonable to assume that if they knew there was a dead Garvey to look for, they'd come to retrieve their ice-pick, left sticking in his chest.

It was time for my daring escape over the rooftops, only there were no rooftops to hand. The whole of Anastasia's upstairs had been knocked into one room, a room with only one window which looked out over the yard. There was no exit that way unless I wanted to break both legs and my pancreas on the paving stones below, so when the footsteps started up the stairs I did the natural thing, climbing up onto Garvey's dressing-table and thence on to the top of his four-poster bed, which was, if I may say so, a particularly fine one, though in bad repair. One day when I have a big house I too will have a four-poster. Garvey's was just a little bigger than my entire bed-sit in Earls Court, Britain, so obviously it was no use to me. It was also very dirty and dusty, like the rest of Anastasia Antiques, and I had an uncomfortable feeling that the sagging frame might give way and deposit me on top of Garvey's blue and gold bedspread with the double-headed eagles, but at least it provided a temporary refuge.

'You'd better be sure,' said someone, in a nasty brogue. 'If there's any slip up in this there'll be hell to pay.'

Somebody else laughed and said, 'Eternal fire?' Another nasty brogue, by which I mean that it belonged to a peasant-type villain, one of the bhoys. Actually the accent had a nice lilt, it was the atmosphere that got me.

Garvey had been a filthy beast because there was a roll of wallpaper and a bucket there on top of the bed, not to mention a lot of dust and a red, white, and blue football rattle inscribed 'World Cup '66'. He must have been a boy at heart, despite his grim exterior and the decadent family background. We could have talked about Sir Alf if I'd known. I am, and ever have been, a Sir Alf fan.

Squirming round the side of the bucket and bracing my shoulders against the ceiling I was able to catch a glimpse of the head and shoulders of the newcomer, which didn't do me a lot of good, because I didn't know him from Adam.

Commit to memory, I thought. Pale face. Crew cut. Then I thought he couldn't be that small, and squirmed a bit more, but he was, and bow-legged like a jockey. He stood at the top of the stairs peering into the room.

11

'There's nothing up here,' he said. 'No sign of him at all.'

'Make sure Sam,' said his confederate.

'I got him all right,' Small Sam said. 'He could hardly crawl upstairs could he?'

'Well he's not below.'

'Come out of that,' Sam said, without much enthusiasm, still not coming into the room.

Well I wasn't fool enough to fall for that one, even if the invitation had been intended for me. I felt reasonably safe on top of Garvey's four-poster, despite the dust in my throat.

'Come on,' Small Sam said, 'the game's up.'

Not a muscle did I move.

'He's not up here,' Small Sam called down the stairs, foiled by my infinite cunning and agility. I don't suppose they reckoned the ice-picked Garvey a good four-poster-climbing prospect.

'Did you *look*, Sam?'

'Otley must have taken him away,' Sam said sourly.

My fingers tightened on the rattle. Otley must have taken him away! I was part of somebody's great plan, which is always unpleasant when you don't know whose plan or what part. Could Small Sam be for Britain?

'You'd better get on with it then,' said Sam's confederate.

'What's the point,' Sam said. 'There's nothing to burn.'

'We don't have to tell Eternity that,' said the voice.

Small Sam picked up a blue watering-can he'd brought up the stairs with him and started sprinkling the floor.

I began to feel a little worried, not to say distressed. I discounted the theory about Sam coming from Alice and M.2. He wasn't our sort of person, he had dandruff and a chest wheeze, and was underweight for his size, about four foot nothing. The National Health would have had him on roast beef right away, if only to justify their existence.

But it wasn't his health that concerned me, it was what he was at with the watering-can. He finished sprinkling and put it down, then he walked to the door.

'Right?' he shouted downstairs.

'Okay.'

Small Sam took a match from his pocket, struck it on the side of one of Garvey's antique slot machines and dropped it on the floor, just as I caught my first whiff of petrol.

The next moment the floor was alight and the curtains smouldering. Sam had fled for his life, and I decided that I wasn't going to be far behind him, having a marked objection to being burnt alive.

I scrambled onto the dressing-table, sending Garvey's 'Bodymist' flying, together with a leather-bound copy of the 'Kama Sutra'.

There was a solid wall of flame between me and the door so it had to be the window, and to hell with my pancreas, dearly as I love it.

So I grabbed the smouldering eagles off the bed and wrapped them round me, then I dashed in the general direction of where the window used to be before the smoke came. It was, in a way, no surprise when I tripped over the electric fire and slammed my head against the wall, but that didn't make it any less

13

upsetting. When I did find the window it wouldn't go up, so I had no alternative but to go through it, head first and in a hurry, Imperial bedspread and all.

I landed with a terrible thud on Garvey's red plastic dustbin in the yard below. It was just as well for me that I did because otherwise I would probably have broken my neck. As it was I only split the plastic bin, and that was in the process of melting anyway.

I poked my head cautiously out of the bedspread. The whole place was on fire, so there was no point in going after my market bag.

Getaway, I thought, and headed for the yard gate. Then I thought about the body I was leaving behind me, which might or might not be consumed in the flames. I decided I'd better take it with me, as a sop to Alice who wasn't going to like the loss of our H.Q. in the Republic.

So I opened the yard gate and dashed back to the van with my handkerchief over my face to stop me from choking. I wrenched the door open and clambered in, very worried in case it would go on fire with me in it.

'Vikdor wants to see you,' said the lady who was sitting at the wheel.

CHAPTER TWO

'Oh yes,' I said, cunningly, as we cruised through side streets in the general direction of O'Connell Street. 'Vikdor does, does he?'

It did seem to me that I was owed an explanation. With the death of Garvey all M.2's Dublin property was temporarily in my care, along with their interests. I didn't know if she was one of Garvey's agents or not, and it bothered me.

'Vikdor doesn't like to be kept waiting,' she said, gruffly. She had a deep voice and a marked Cork accent.

Well, bully for Vikdor. Whether Vikdor was pro or anti Garvey was probably the question of the hour, but I didn't know how to phrase it tactfully. The lady wasn't training a luger on me so it seemed that I was probably on her side, and therefore Vikdor's.

I don't think we've met before, Mr. Garvey,' she said. 'My name is Maggie Keough.'

'Delighted,' I said, swiftly deciding that if she thought I was Garvey I'd better be him. Garvey was supposed to be Our Man in Dublin, in M.2 circles, but it was always possible that he'd been mixing his allegiances, in which case saying I wasn't him but I was M.2 might prove unfortunate, though she didn't look particularly deadly. She was brown skinned like a turf-cutter's daughter, the wrong side of forty, with a misapplied purple tint that didn't help her bouffant hair-do. She wore a rough tweed jacket and corduroy trousers, and there was enough of her in evidence to convince me that she wasn't Grace in disguise, though Grace habitually turns up dressed as boneyard-type ladies. She smelt strongly of pine trees and tobacco smoke, which I put down to inclination rather than environment.

'You don't mind if I drive?' she said.

'All right,' I said, as we headed in the direction of the bridge. I needed a breathing space, so I thought I'd relax and prepare myself for whatever excitement was to follow.

It was a basic mistake. She hadn't taken her driving test on a sidecar by any means, she was a second Fangio, born with a Ferrari in the stables, alongside the churn and the buttermilk.

'Don't worry,' she said. 'I know this route like the back of my hand.' We skidded round St. Stephen's Green, revved the engine in Merrion Row and disappeared in a cloud of dust up the Baggot Streets, Lower and Upper, which were gone before I had time to notice them. I could hear poor dead Garvey bumping about like nobody's business in the back, getting all tangled up with the sten gun.

'Couldn't we slow down a little?' I said, as we screamed past Ballsbridge.

'Don't worry chummy,' she said, putting her foot down.

'You can open your eyes now,' she said, some fifteen minutes later.

16

I released my hand hold on the ashtray, glad that I was going to live to visit the Joyce Museum after all.

The ground came up to meet me, but I took firm control of myself and staggered in the general direction of what turned out to be a sea wall whilst a playful wind did its best to decimate me.

'My tummy feels funny,' I gasped, courageously. Well it did, and I thought she ought to know about it, as it was all her fault.

She was already standing on top of the wall, her corduroys sagging at the knees, her stout leather shoes with the metal tips ringing against the stones. She gave me a hand up, without which I would never have made it.

'Thank you,' I said.

'Have a rest chummy,' she said. 'Bit of bluster will put the puff in you,' Her bit of a bluster was my playful wind living up to its potential and threatening to blow me away. She beamed at me. 'Not been in the forces, have you?' she said, 'That'd make a man of you.'

I felt that my dignity called for a display of virile sprightliness, just show her what we C.N.D. boys are made of. So I jumped off the sea wall, instead of walking along it to the steps. It turned out to be a nine-foot drop.

'Hurt yourself?' she said, standing over me as I lay in agony on the shingle.

I gritted my teeth and said I was all right thank you.

'We'd better get busy,' she said.

I waited politely for what came next. She took off her jacket and blouse, and I didn't flinch. She was

17

wearing a canvas corset which she unwound and handed to me. Then she put her blouse back on again, took her corset back, and removed the canisters from the little pockets strung around it, taking eight for herself and giving eight to me.

'Half each,' she said, by way of explanation.

It didn't help me much. Garvey might have known what to do with them, but I hadn't a clue. I was tempted to make off over the sands, leaving her to it, but I had a horrible and not unjustified suspicion that she might catch and clobber me if I tried, not unconnected with the metal-tipped shoes, which can be very nasty things if you're so minded.

I was beginning to regret having missed the opportunity of disowning Garvey's identity, especially as he was tangled up with the sten gun in the back of the van. If she or this Vikdor person happened to look inside, I was going to have to explain him, which might not be easy. There was also no guarantee that Vikdor would accept my new identity as easily as Maggie Keough had.

Worried, I followed her on what turned out to be a route march over the sands. Several minutes later she turned aside and set off walking in a wide arc, putting down her canisters at even intervals, so I took my cue and moved in a wide arc opposite hers. Then I noticed that her canisters were shining in the night and mine weren't, so I had to back track and fiddle with them until they went on.

'Very pretty,' I said, hoping it would appease her, as she seemed a little impatient at the time I'd taken.

She offered me a puff of her cigarette, which I thought a little odd, but accepted, for fear that it was a national custom. One has to keep in with the natives.

'Does you good,' she said.

'Yes,' I said, and inhaled deeply.

It was pot. I don't hold with pot, so I stopped smoking it quickly. Pot, circles on the sand. We were going to hold a black mass.

'Where,' I said, still a little lightheaded from my puff, 'Where is Long Thom?'

She was about to answer when we heard a whirring noise. She stubbed her ciggy out and stuffed it inside her kinky corset. 'Vikdor doesn't approve,' she said, rebuttoning her blouse.

The whirring sound grew louder and my agile mind arrived at the correct reason for the lighted circle. We were a temporary heliport. We drew back some way and waited as the helicopter nestled down on the sand, and the blades stopped rotating.

'Out you go,' she said, 'and mind your tongue.'

I walked out over the sands towards the dark shape of the helicopter, not feeling too happy about life. Someone had climbed down from it and was standing waiting for me, an impressively tall man in a black leather overcoat.

'Garvey?' he said.

'That's it,' I said, taking my life in my hands.

There was an uneasy silence.

'Come for a walk,' he said.

So we did, out by the tide, with the wind flapping our clothes and far too much ozone for my delicate constitution, but it didn't seem to worry the mysterious Vikdor at all.

'You are not as I expected you to be,' he said, after

19

we'd walked a little. 'I had expected an older man.'
Well that was hardly surprising, considering I wasn't
Garvey. 'You're a good advertisement for the service,'
he said.

'In a manner of speaking,' I said.

'They have a customer on the morning plane,' he
said. 'Everard, another American. I'd like you to look
out for him if you will. I understand he's not what he
seems, but Eternity don't know that. I want to know
what happens to him, just in case we decide to risk
one of our own.'

'Yes,' I said, as the damp seeped through my
shoes, which had been in need of repair for some
time.

'They'll have someone there to meet him, but we
understand that he'll be carrying a copy of the New
Testament in paperback, so he shouldn't be hard to
pick out. Naturally you won't be expected, and there
is no reason why you should let either Everard or his
escort know that you're interested, so don't interfere.
If the Americans want to investigate Eternity well
and good; we can always close in after they get results,
if they get them. Just keep an eye on what happens,
in particular where they take him to and who he
meets.'

'Ah yes,' I said, 'Eternity,' the idea was that he
would pick up the subject and expound, but he
didn't, which I thought a little mean of him, considering that I was supposed to be on his side. By this
time my socks were wringing wet.

'I believe you had a spot of bother tonight,' he said.
'It came over the phones.'

'Yes,' I said, giving him a bit of his own back.

'I assume,' he said, 'that it was in your British capacity?'

'I imagine so,' I said.

'Don't get too involved with the British,' he said. 'We would not like to be forced to remind you of the priorities of the profession.'

Filthy woggies, I thought, meaning both Garvey and Vikdor, who had obviously been dealing in M.2's secrets at their leisure. 'I know the priorities,' I said, with skilful ambiguity.

'If anything went wrong,' he said, 'we would know exactly how to cope with the situation. The wrong name on the wrong telephone, the one with the additional listener. Eternity would do the rest, and I don't think any of us would underestimate Eternity.'

It was all a bit beyond me, but I smiled politely and ground my chattering teeth together. Mercifully, he started back towards the helicopter. We walked in silence towards it, and paused by its side.

'I'm glad to have met you, Garvey,' he said. 'I'm sure you'll do a good job for us on this one. Whatever happens, remember that Everard is expendable, he doesn't work for us. Is that plain?'

'Yes,' I said.

Then he clambered up into the helicopter and I started back across the sand thinking how proud Alice was going to be of my role in the night's skull-duggery.

Vikdor was no more than a distant whirr when I reached Fangio-in-skirts who was sitting on the wall puffing her pot. She offered me a go, but I refused. I wouldn't have taken her for a flower person, which shows how wrong you can be.

'Where to?' she asked, heading for the driving seat.
'Town,' I said, 'but I'll drive.'

So it was that I came to be bedless in Dublin at four
o'clock in the morning with a dead Garvey and a sten
gun in the back of my van and a problem about
Eternity, which, for want of a better hypothesis, I
took to be an illegal organisation.

I watched Maggie Keough striding away from the
van and set my mind on the necessity for action.

Phonebox, I thought, ring Alice. I was supposed to
be in Anastasia's standing by, but as Anastasia's was
no longer there to stand by in, my duty was to get in
touch and give her the bad news about the way
Vikdor had been running rings round us.

'London Management,' said the weary voice on the
London end of the phone, after I'd finished my customary quarrel with the operator.

'Miss Alexander,' I said.

'Who is that please?'

'Gerald Otley,' I said, 'O-T-L-E-Y, Otley.'

I could sense hesitation at the other end, it wasn't
the first time I'd had a clash of personalities with the
morning-girl. Once there had been an unfortunate
conversation between us when I'd rung up from one
of Charles' parties about a money order Alice had
forgotten to send me.

'It's a bit late isn't it?' she said.

'Listen,' I said, 'I'll have you know I'm now head of
operations in Dublin. Didn't the night operator tell
you?'

'No,' she said. Then I heard her say to someone.
'Shall I put him through? It's that rude little man

22

after money again.' There followed a terse mumble and a laugh.

'Hullo, headquarters Dublin?' said the shrewd voice. 'Are you still there?'

'Please be quick,' I said.

'Hope it's a good party,' she said.

I thought it was time to pull a little rank. 'Miss Alexander will be most upset if you do not attend to me immediately,' I said. 'Time is of the essence.'

'Putting you through *sir*,' she shrilled, 'But don't ask for money again, she'll kill you.'

There was a click and a voice said: 'At the third stroke it will be four ten and thirty seconds.'

'Hullo Alice,' I said.

Peep peep peep went the phone.

I heard the sound of distant laughter and put down the receiver with such dignity as was left to me. That morning girl at M.2 had it coming! There would come a day when the name of Otley would strike dread in her heart. Communication was obviously hopeless until the day girl came on, so I had to fight on single-handed.

I sat down in a shop doorway and thought, being somewhat exhausted. It was already almost daylight and the prospects of slipping Garvey's corpse into the Liffey and remaining unseen were now very slight. I was very tired, my feet were icy, and there was nothing positive that I could do until the changeover of telephonists when I had to ring Alice and ask her whether I was to follow the expendable Everard or not.

Home through the morning streets, with something of the dread of an early worm.

Imogen lives in South Anne Street, whence I made my way, directing myself as usual by the Liffey and the statues. I climbed the stairs to her flat and rang the bell loudly.

'Hullo,' she said. She was dressed in old jeans and a string sweater, with ballet pumps on her feet. She is a very advanced lady, having left her convent far behind her.

'I'm sorry if I got you out of bed,' I said, bearing in mind that it was twenty to five.

'I've been feeding the birds,' she said.

I collapsed on the sofa, feeling pathetic.

'Tea?' she asked.

'Something stronger,' I said.

She went away to get it. I picked up her discarded packet of birdseed and idly started nibbling, just to see if it would turn me on. I was half way through when I happened to catch sight of the label.

'FOREVER BIRD', and in small letters just by the tear-tab, 'An Eternity Product'.

CHAPTER THREE

I skulked over O'Connell bridge, watching the Liffey
slip by me, on my reluctant way to the Busarus.
Around me Dublin streamed, talking maps talked,
blue and yellow buses whipped to and fro and statues
gesticulated. People darted across roads as though
they'd never heard of being run over. It was, of
course, drizzling, but at least that gave me the
authentic espionage atmosphere.

Thwarted was the word. Bandy Alice was in conference, and there was no message for me at M.2. The
van was still where I'd left it, so for the moment
Garvey would just have to take his chance with the
rest of us. I'd gone carefully over it the night before,
wiping off the fingerprints, so if anybody chanced
upon him there was nothing to connect either corpse
or sten gun with me, and if the van stayed undis-
turbed I could come back under cover of darkness
and drive him down to the river, a dash and a splash
and a watery grave. As to my personal affairs, they
were in ruins. I was supposed to be in Dublin buying
for Chloe, and Chloe wasn't going to be pleased when
she found out that I'd been neglecting her interests.
As soon as somebody from M.2 arrived I was going to
hand over the whole thing to them, and get on with
my own good works. Chloe has a lot of influence,

being Heindleighter's aunt. It would never do to cross her.

I turned aside and walked down dismal Eden Quay and round the back of the Customs House, wondering if I was doing the right thing. It was most unreasonable, I should have had a clear directive from London. It was plain to me that Alice thought I was safe inside Anastasia's, and was taking her time, but I couldn't seem to get the message through, even to the day girl. After a struggle with myself I had decided at least to go to the Busarus and take a look at the incoming passengers, to see if Everard-with-the-New-Testament really existed. There was also the chance of a look at the Man from Eternity, whatever Eternity was, apart from a birdseed business.

I had a feeling that I was up to no good.

At one of the kiosks inside the Busarus I took my time about buying a postcard with a Leprechaun to send to Chloe, telling her I was concentrating on her needs to the exclusion of all, and how much I wished she was here, fat old bag. Any relative of Heindleighter's is a potential enemy of mine, but worth keeping in with for reasons of high finance. I was all right so long as Chloe didn't mention me to Heidie, which would mean the end of everything.

Then the airport bus came purring in. Twenty-three people got off, among them a slight man in a white raincoat, clutching a copy of the New Testament.

He set off round Beresford Place and into Lower Abbey Street as though butter wouldn't melt in his mouth. A small man in a lush tweed suit set off after him and I set off after the small man, on the principle that if it interested Vikdor, M.2 would probably like to know.

The Abbey was playing 'Shadow of a Gunman', which I thought apt, but neither of them took any notice, which showed the calibre of person I was mixing with. We crossed O'Connell Street and turned down the quays past a lovely bookshop where I paused for a moment to inspect a copy of 'God in the Garden', whilst the Man from Eternity pulled abreast of the expendable Everard. They paused on the metal bridge and stood there chatting like old chums.

I came slowly on, hoping for a closer look, but before I was anywhere near them they started off again, crossing the bridge and nipping through a dark archway past a little man who was sketching it for posterity.

Over the metal bridge at a gallop I went, and three buses blocked my way on the other side, an unexpected irritant. So I nipped between them, and a man on a bicycle nearly killed me, with the very best of intentions, by which I mean that he wasn't in it professionally, he was just bad at bicycling.

Round the sketcher and through the archway I dashed, and out into Temple Bar, which was unexpectedly empty. No sign of either of them. I darted up the alley opposite the arch and through another one. A sign on the wall said that I couldn't go any further unless I was a member of the Chamber of Commerce, but I risked my all and kept going into a courtyard where bleak and dusty apartments looked down on passing commerce, three mini-skirts and me at that moment. On I went through the building on the other side and out into Dame Street. In the distance Thomas Davis beckoned, at home with the tin things in his puddle.

I stood where I was, cross. My day for losing people had obviously come unless, of course, they had conspired to lose me.

'Damn,' I said, and a passing lady crossed herself with fervour, and forgave me.

A dingy sign above my head said 'Ouzel Bar'. Alas how the good days had passed it by. When I was in Dublin with American Julian we had our morning drinks in the Ouzel, along with all the poets. Now the dear old Ouzel was no more. The spirit of its poetry lived on in me, I assured it silently, but just then I wasn't in the mood for composition.

I sat in the Daid with Imogen, feeling a failure in espionage. Bandy Alice had placed Anastasia's in my care, the mysterious Vikdor had given me an invaluable lead to I knew not what, and I'd muffed both assignments, as Anastasia's had been burnt to the ground and expendable Everard had vanished into thin air.

'Tell me,' I said, somewhat drunkenly, 'What is Eternity?'

A small gentleman rose from his seat and went to stand at the bar, looking upset.

'Eternity,' replied Imogen, equally drunkenly, in fact more so, 'is a sort of birdseed.'

We considered this proposition together. It seemed accurate but unsatisfactory.

'It does seem to me,' I said, with furrowed brows. 'That there is mayhap more to Eternity than birdseed.'

But Imogen had gone to sleep. It was all of twelve o'clock in the morning, but then she'd had a difficult night with the birds, who were supposed to be sitting on their current egg, but were flunking out on duty. Fantail pigeons have no sense of responsibility, you've got to be on at them about it all the time. The FOR-EVER BIRD was by way of a bribe, but it hadn't gone down very well. Actually I'd eaten most of it myself as an experiment, which had caused a small rift in our relationship. I respect Imogen's intellect, but find her relationship with her birds a little unhealthy, smacking of the cloisters whence she came.

I went down the steep stairs to the lavatory, immortalised in the 'Ginger Man' but a trap for the unwary innocent for all that. In civilisation they'd have had a lift and kept the steps as a monument. On the way back up ... the *long* way back up ... I bumped into the small man who had been by the bar.

'Sir,' I said, politely, 'watch the step.'

'What do you know about Eternity?' he asked.

'Eternity is a sort of birdseed,' I stated firmly, glad to find a common ground with the cultural élite.

'That is true,' he said.

'Eternity is also something else,' I said, tapping him firmly on the waistcoat. 'I don't yet know what, but I'm dedicated to finding out for Alice.'

'How?' he said.

I looked crafty. 'Let us go to the bar,' I said.

We went to the bar and he bought me a drink, which I thought was awfully good of him. All the best people go to the Daid, but they don't always buy you drinks.

29

'I know something that Eternity doesn't,' I said. 'I'm on to all the dodges.'

'Oh?' he said, and I sensed disbelief.

'Listen,' I said, carefully sitting myself down on one of their little red stools. 'Vikdor told me.'

In some magic way the glass in front of me had re-filled itself. I thanked it very much.

'What did Vikdor tell you?' the little man asked.

'About Everard,' I said. 'They don't know it, but Everard is expendable.'

Then I noticed that Imogen had wakened up again. 'Come here and talk to this nice man, Imogen,' I cried, and she came.

But by the time she got to us, he had gone away.

A man in a white bar-coat put a plate down in front of me.

'What's this?' I asked. 'I never ordered this.'

'Ham sandwich,' he said.

Oh well, I thought, it certainly looked appetising. Never look a gift ham in the mouth, I thought, and told Imogen about it, and she thought it was really extremely funny.

So I lifted the lovely sandwich and was about to take a bite when I noticed the card that had been slipped beneath it. On one side was the name 'Percy Smith, Central Representative' and on the other 'Eternity is the FOREVER drink'.

The afternoon sun beat down mercilessly on the doorway of the Daïd, where I stood supporting Imogen and she stood supporting me.

'Home,' I said, conscious that someone had to take charge of a rapidly deteriorating situation.

Somehow we negotiated Grafton Street and started up South Anne Street, making a detour to avoid a nun with a little tin.

Much as I'd expected, there was a large man in a black coat standing in the doorway of Imogen's home.

'Walk straight past,' I hissed to Imogen, but she giggled and kept straight on going, till she bumped into him. The man picked her off his chest and propped her against the post-box. Then he caught my arm and pulled me back. 'Afternoon sir,' he said. He had a hat, and round the hat was a yellow band which read 'Eternity Services'. I ignored his presence diplomatically, on the wishful theory that he might be a mirage, a theory which did not allow for the large hand that was bruising my biceps. 'Came to pick you up sir,' he said, respectfully, but with a no-nonsense look in his eye.

'Go away,' I said, summoning all the authority I could muster.

He turned me round and steered me towards the sort of Rolls Royce you associate with the Queen Mother and the Lord Mayor, even to the little flag on the front.

'Imogen,' I cried. 'Help!'

Either she didn't hear me, or she didn't want to know. She closed the door shakily behind her after giving me an inane grin, on her way back to the feckless fantails upstairs. My friend Grace would have rushed in to help me, but Imogen was no Grace.

'In you get sir,' he said, manhandling me forward, so that I landed on the back seat of the Rolls Royce, a circumstance I normally would have found most gratifying, being a natural aristocrat. But the hot blood in my veins was all a-bubble, so I started trying to get out, vigorously kicking the door, from which the inside handle had been removed. I hurt my foot, but the door didn't budge.

So I beat frantically on the windowglass as we cruised past the nun, but she was concentrating on a small child with a shilling, and paid me no attention. Normally I'm pro-nun, but I sat back feeling decidedly anti.

I began to feel groggy. It could have been the drink, but it didn't feel like that kind of groggy, so I sat still and tried to think what kind of groggy it might be.

It was then that I noticed the faint hissing sound, and the sickly sweet smell.

Investigate, I thought, but I couldn't find anything to investigate except the rubber monkey that hung on the back window, and it seemed inoffensive if ugly. I dismissed the monkey from my calculations.

Pull back the driver's partition, I thought, demand to be let out at once.

So I tried pulling back the partition, but it wouldn't pull. I couldn't work out whether it wouldn't pull because I was too weak to pull it, or whether it wouldn't pull because it wouldn't pull. So I gave up trying to pull it and somehow found myself lying on the floor of the moving car. You've got to show dignity in a Rolls because of the export market, so I gritted my teeth and levered myself up, heading for the seat, feeling very very sleepy and rather happy.

I got myself upright, with my head lolling beside the rubber monkey which had a little green hat and a yellow jacket. It bobbed up and down, quite capturing my attention. Clever, I thought.

The monkey was doing the hissing. But rubber monkeys don't hiss, it just isn't done.

'Nice monkey,' I said, feeling sleepy.

It finally penetrated to my fuddled brain that the back of the Rolls was airtight and that the funny smell and the monkey's soothing hiss indicated gas.

I made a last move for the door, but didn't make it. Instead I found myself letting down the British image and lying on the floor coughing, with only the monkey's hiss to entertain me. I felt quite happy in a way, because it was *a Rolls,* and therefore a distinctively U way to go.

CHAPTER FOUR

I had an idea that I might be dead, which came as rather a shock, especially as my last pertinent thought on the subject had been the anti-nun one which mightn't go down well where I was going. The other place was definitely out, being packed to the doors with Heindleighter's relations.

It hurt to open my eyes, but I did it because I couldn't stand the suspense which was, as I deftly phrased it, killing me. Opening my eyes didn't do me much good, because all was darkness, impregnated with a strong smell of cat.

My C. of E. heaven couldn't possibly smell of cat, I reasoned triumphantly, so I was alive, but apart from that there was nothing to justify hysterical laughter. I had a sore head and a filthy taste in my mouth, which seemed likely to be connected with it. Then I remembered my ride in Eternity's mobile gas-chamber and the hours in the Daid which had preceded it, put two and two together and congratulated myself on survival.

Sit very still, I thought, you'll feel better in a minute. Well I didn't, at least not much, but my indomitable courage carried me forward for a cautious grope, by way of exploring my surroundings.

I established that I was sitting on a deckchair when I got my finger caught in it. Then I pushed forward and touched a curving wooden surface. Follow it to the door, I thought, and got to my feet to grope along it. I'd been twice round it before I realised that I was walking round in circles, with my deckchair as the centrepoint. So I went back and sat on my deckchair partly because I was dizzy and partly because I'd lost faith in my legs.

I couldn't understand it at all. I was at the mercy of something called Eternity, purveyors of birdseed and stout and gassy Rolls Royces, the subject of an investigation by the American Intelligence people and the avid interest of Vikdor. They were probably foul, but they meant nothing to me and I couldn't understand why I should mean anything to them. What had they got against me? Then I thought about it a bit more and remembered my talkative friend who gave away ham sandwiches.

Light flooded in from the doorway for which I had searched so fruitlessly. It was a perfect fit, good, I suppose, for gassing, if you had an inclination that way.

'Out you get,' somebody said, so I got out.

It was the small man from the Daid, who was no doubt responsible for my troubles. I stood looking at him with a friendly smile on my face to indicate that it was all a mistake.

'Where am I?' I asked.

'In the brewery,' he said.

'What brewery?' I said.

'Eternity Stout,' he said.

'Oh,' I said.

'We haven't time for a tour or I'd take you round,' he said, affably. 'We like to give people the right impression, it's good for the image. As it is you've had a close up view of our oldest cask, and that'll have to do you a while.'

So I'd slept it off in a cask, after being gassed by the monkey in their lovely Rolls. If that was their image I wasn't impressed.

'Are you in the habit of keeping innocent people in casks?' I said, bitterly. Well, I had reason to be bitter. 'I have reason to be *bitter*,' I said, but he didn't get it. I marked the quip down to tell Imogen, always assuming I got out of the brewery alive.

'Yes,' he said, an answer which was a trifle off-putting, but probably honest. Then he said would I mind getting on the train.

I thought he was being funny and was about to try my bitter line again in a new variation when I saw that there was a train, if only a tiny one, like Battersea without the Emmett Engine, for this one was strictly work-a-day. So I climbed onto the train and he started the engine. We whirred off along a narrow railway.

'Diesel,' he said, in reply to my unspoken question, which had remained unspoken because I was chiefly concerned with my tummy, which was a trifle upset. 'We are very up-to-date at Eternity.'

I asked him what about casks that smelt of cat. He said that the cask was a tourist attraction and the cat wasn't on the strength. Then we whirred out into the open air, across a narrow yard, and down a tunnel into a loading bay. He helped me out of the train, which was a relief, because I'd been getting the

36

bends sitting with my legs screwed up in the tiny carriage.

'What's this all in aid of?' I said.

'Shutting your mouth,' he said, somewhat grimly. 'If necessary ... forever.'

Then he ushered me into a small office, haphazardly furnished and ill lit, the walls decorated with loading schedules and naked ladies and a newspaper cutting about a nun in Wicklow. She was fully clothed, so she must have been somebody's sister. He sat me down in a swivel chair and I admired their ink wells which had come out of the Ark.

'Boss'll be in in a minute,' he said.

Then the boss came in.

'This is...' my friend began, but the newcomer shushed him.

'Otley of M.2.,' he said.

It was Garvey ... Garvey, but Garvey was dead, so it couldn't be Garvey. But it *was* Garvey.

'You can't be Garvey,' I said. 'Garvey's dead. I saw him at Anastasia's.'

He smiled politely and sat down, flexing massive gloved hands on the desk before him and looking as if he was enjoying himself. 'Nonetheless I'm here,' he said. 'You must make up your mind about that.'

I pointed out that he couldn't be here, not after being dead. It seemed a reasonable point of view, yet I put it without much confidence.

'I'm one of the swine who live forever,' he said. 'The privileged few, you understand. You could put it down to the stout.'

'Don't give me that,' I said, indignantly.

He shrugged. 'You've seen me dead, now you see me alive. Either your eyes are playing tricks or . . . and I'd like you to think about it . . . I have been brought back.'

'Either my eyes are playing tricks *or* you're not Garvey at all,' I said, triumphantly.

'M.2 gave you one of their little print slips on me, I suppose?' he said. 'Alice is usually thorough that way.' He took off his glove and flapped it at me.

With misgiving, I fished out the cellophane slip with the fingerprints of M.2's man in Dublin on it. He stuck his fingers in the desk ink pad and pressed firmly down on the edge of an order slip. Then he tore it off and the two fitted exactly, allowing for a little blurring.

'I'm here to scare the hell out of you Mr. Otley,' he said. 'We don't want you sticking your nose in our affairs. I could rub you out,' he said, fitting the glove back on, 'like that . . . scrub, scrub. But I don't like working that way. You've proved harmless, if loud-mouthed, so far. Here at Eternity we are more concerned with preserving life than destroying it . . . we don't often have to resort to violence. You must believe me, when I suggest to you that you would be wise to pack up and go . . . we simply will not tolerate being interfered with.'

I smiled politely.

'You don't take us very seriously do you?' he said.

'Frankly, no,' I said, intimating, which was quite true, that I was used to dealing with the international set.

'I could . . .' he started, and then stopped. 'But there are things you have no need to know. Let's put it this way. We have unlimited resources at our disposal. Those who would not die ... ever ... have a price to pay. They pay it. For the remainder ... let us say we're developing as a destructive force.'

'But of course,' I said.

'We have our own...' he began, and then seemed to have second thoughts about it. I waited politely. 'You'll be hearing more about us, never fear,' he said.

'I'm sure,' I said, glibly.

'Get out of Dublin,' he said. 'You're to tell Alice I'm dead. You don't know anything else about it ... is that clear? I don't want M.2 fussing about. You have twenty-four hours to get out ... and if you don't, or if you talk too much ... steps will be taken.'

'I haven't got the fare,' I said, ever practical.

'Mr. Smith will give you your plane ticket on the way out,' he said. 'First class, of course.'

The little man from the Daid let me out into the street again.

'Poor old chap,' he said, 'you look a bit shaken. Look, if you need any help about settling things here before you go, don't hesitate to ring me at the brewery. Percy Smith is the name, you'll find our number in the book.'

'I met you in the Daid,' I said. 'Didn't I?'

He said he was glad I'd got the sandwich, and closed the gate, leaving me looking at a big sign that said: ETERNITY IS A JOY FOREVER.

Overhead the moon shone down on the cobbles of the deserted street. I started to walk Imogen-wards, feeling limp. There was something horribly impressive about an organisation that didn't put you up against a brick wall and shoot you. They obviously assumed that they were so well known and so terrifying that they only had to say go away and I'd go. As a procedure, it was almost unethical. Then there was the problem of dead Garvey, sitting there chatting. The implications of that were pretty terrifying, *if it really was Garvey.*

I had seen Garvey. I had talked to Garvey. But Garvey was dead. Therefore it couldn't possibly be Garvey. So it was somebody dressed up as Garvey. After all, I didn't know Garvey very well. We'd never met in the flesh, all I'd seen were Bandy Alice's photographs from the file. So the impostor only had to look like Garvey to fool me. But he knew about me, and in Dublin only Garvey could know. Then logic rescued me ... Garvey had told them about me. They'd worked a similar trick on him before they did him in, and he'd fallen for it, and spilled the beans. There remained the awkward fact of the fingerprints to dispose of.

I still had one card up my sleeve, and that was the real Garvey lying dead in the van, wrapped round the sten gun. So I changed course from Imogen's and went to check if he was still where I'd left him.

The van was there, but no Garvey.

Keep cool, I thought. They'd moved the corpse. Fair enough. If they knew about the trip to the seaside they would also know where I'd parked when I got back. The fact that my Garvey was gone didn't prove that their live one was my dead one warmed up. What I needed was somebody who really knew Garvey.

Alice of M.2. Phone Alice.

I started off for the phonebox, then spotted one on the other side of the road that I'd missed the night before, which saved me five minutes walk.

I gave the peasant the number and waited for the argument.

'I don't know about this,' he said, true to form.

'Hurry,' I said, 'this is urgent.'

'Do you think I should?' he said.

'What do you mean?' I snapped, not tolerating any back-chat from rebellious peasants. Personally I find it difficult to trust a bullet-scarred post office, but that was their affair. Back-chat from peasant operators was something else again.

'Well,' the peasant said. 'Eternity won't like it, will they?'

I replaced the receiver with a shaking hand. They had got the Post Office Telephone Service. Maybe it was all true. Maybe Garvey was back from the dead. But you can't bring people back from the dead ... can you?

Back to Imogen's for solace, and to find out what she thought about it. It was, after all, her Post Office.

It took me ten minutes to get back to Imogen's, by which time I'd worked myself up into a pretty firm conviction that every lamp-post was in the pay of Eternity, not to speak of Thomas Davis and his tin things, which seemed to swivel after me.

I opened the door of Imogen's, to find that she'd left the light on on the stairs, which was very careless of her. Imogen's is a pretty odd place anyway, being a tiny penthouse on top of the offices of a brand of cat-food hideously advertised on the side walls. The point of the penthouse is to give her somewhere for her birds to fly in and out of, which makes it cosy for the birds but very chill for everyone else, as I'd found out to my acute discomfort.

Imogen's front door was wide open, which isn't like her either.

'Imogen!' I called, standing in the hall with my shoes in my hand.

She did not answer.

Then I had a nasty thought. Eternity had got her, just to show me they meant business. They would send me her ear in a cigar box. Or if not Eternity, then Maggie Keough and Leather Vikdor who had found out I wasn't Garvey.

I sprinted up the stairs, and banged on her door.

Not a whisper.

So I threw the door open, dramatically, prepared to sob on the sheets if it was called for.

She was in bed, and apparently fast asleep.

Bed seemed a good idea. Eternity could wait till the morning. I was quite exhausted going over the possibilities of a stout firm who'd arrived at the secret of keeping people alive when they should have been dead. I was sick of it all, and confused. Maybe Imogen could have helped sort it out, if she'd been awake, but there was no point in disturbing her, because once Imogen is asleep, she's asleep.

So I got into my pyjamas and climbed into bed beside her.

'Hullo,' she murmured sleepily.

'Hullo dear,' I said, affectionately.

'You're very late,' she said.

Well she *was* wide-awake, for her. Normally a grunt was as much as you got, when she'd managed to forget about the birds long enough to get over. 'You're quite a mimic,' I said. 'I used to have a Scots lady friend who talked just like that.'

'Did you, lamb?' she said.

There is only one lady who can call me lamb and get away with it, and it isn't Imogen.

I switched on the bedside lamp.

Grace gave me her familiar two-toothed lip look, an expression which usually indicates that she's been up to some devilment.

'What have you done with Imogen?' I cried.

'Is Imogen,' Grace said, 'the drunken blonde who lives here?'

'Yes,' I said. 'And I demand to know what you've done with her.'

'Oh she's all right,' Grace said. 'I put her in the cupboard.'

CHAPTER FIVE

'I think,' Grace said, 'that it is time we were going.'

I pointed out that Imogen had not yet regained consciousness. She lay draped on the sofa where I'd put her after taking her out of the cupboard. From the way Grace had bundled her up in the first place, I don't think they can have had much in common.

'I hate to think what you did to her,' I said, feeling indignant. I felt a certain responsibility towards Imogen, even if I'd gone off her a bit over the carry-on with the birds. Grace was a nicer lady but she did have an unfortunate side to her character, which I could only term viciousness. 'Imogen,' I said, 'has been very good to me since I've been in Dublin. I can't just leave her semi-conscious on the sofa.'

'I don't see why not,' Grace said, hitching her ski-pants which I must say fitted her remarkably well. She looked all soft and fragile with her hair flouncing round her, the sort to take home to mother except that, in Grace's case, mother would need to be a karate black belt. 'Your lady friend will be fine and dandy when she wakes up,' Grace said cheerfully, and the two rabbit teeth appeared on her lip again, a most attractive expression, but one with unfortunate associations for me. It probably meant that Imogen was going to feel very, very grey indeed.

'So you *say*,' I said.

'I gave her a pill,' Grace said, a little aggrieved.

I said it was some pill that could lay a lady out for as long as poor Imogen had been laid out. She had been out of the cupboard since 3 a.m. and it was now ten o'clock and breakfast time, but still she lay limp and languid, without so much as a twitch.

'I could have been much nastier,' Grace said.

For once, I felt that she was telling the whole truth.

'Well, what sort of pill was it then?' I said, crowding my advantage. But Grace had gone into the kitchen, out of the way.

I went out on to the birds' roof to get some air. It was a splendid morning and I smiled at the passing populace, nibbling the birdseed and feeling like St. Francis.

No birds. Not a twitter from the fantails. The silence was eerie.

The victim of a horrible supposition I sped to their little hutch, fearful of what I might find.

One of them lay flat out beside the egg, the other leered at me, broken in spirit.

'They made too much noise,' Grace said. 'I couldn't get to sleep.'

'This,' I cried, 'is too much.'

Morning coffee in the Oriental Tea-Rooms where I only just averted a disaster, barring Grace by brute force from entering the masculine enclave below. Ladies, I told her, had to stay upstairs. She said she was no lady, she could take on any three of them, given choice of weapons. I said I'd observed as much

45

during our past association, but had refrained from saying so, being a gentleman.

'We are rapier sharp this morning,' she said, fingering a delicious cream cornet she'd got to first. 'Sex must do you good.'

I said if she didn't want to eat the cream cornet she could give it to me. As to sex, I said, Imogen and I had a meeting of the minds. *Not* that I'd ever met her mind, which she kept under the bed, with the whiskey.

'Were you uncomfortable on the cushions?' she said, referring to what had been an unforgivable night, both physically and from the point of view of my dignity. It was something I'd been trying not to think about.

'I think that you are jealous of Imogen,' I said, watching her finish off the cream cornet, 'that's what I think. You fancy me yourself, don't you? All this griping and doping people is just sour grapes.'

She laughed it off, but I didn't believe her. Not for nothing am I renowned in the bistros of Pimlico, the hot chocolate spots of Worlds End.

'To change the subject,' she said, 'what does Eternity mean to you?'

'Birdseed,' I said, impassively.

'My information is that you know rather more than that,' she said, toying with her tea spoon. 'It's obvious to all concerned that there's more to it than birds and stout.

'Such as?' I said.

She handed me a newspaper cutting. NUCLEAR DEVICE RECOVERED, it said in large black letters. The heading read *New York Times*.

'And?' I said.

'My information is that it wasn't,' Grace said. 'Or at least not by U.S. Navy. Other people were looking for it as well.'

'And Eternity...'

'Just happened to have one of their tankers in the vicinity at the time.'

'Oh,' I said.

'It is entirely possible,' Grace said, 'that the nice homespun brewery up the road is now a nuclear power.'

'Oh,' I said.

'Or they may not be. That is the question. That's what I'm here to find out.'

'The nice homespun brewery up the road also claims to bring back the dead,' I said, glad to be able to put my oar in. She looked a little askance as I coolly sipped my oriental coffee.

'This is no joking matter,' she said stiffly.

Neither, I intimated, was dead Garvey.

'I heard about your corpse yesterday,' she said, 'if that's what you're on about. What's that got to do with Eternity?'

'The trouble with yesterday's corpse,' I said, 'is that it wasn't, if you follow me.'

She said something sceptical and I silenced her with a cold glance. Then I explained about Garvey being dead, and then again not being dead, in that he was able to hold menacing confrontations in the offices of Eternity and match up to his own official fingerprints, as provided by the files of M.2.

'You're sure that there was a corpse in the first place?' Grace asked.

47

Stone dead, I said, transfixed with an ice-pick.

'Why pretend to bring people back to life if you can't?' I said. 'And I take it we are agreed that they can't? Unless, of course, they are fiendishly clever.'

'As a working hypothesis,' Grace said, 'let us assume that they are fiendishly clever.'

'But why...' I said. 'What does a brewery want with that sort of thing?'

'Let's stick to the job in hand, shall we?' Grace said. 'Just now whether they can bring people back from the dead or not doesn't seem very important to me.'

I said I couldn't help worrying about it all the same.

She said I should worry about an expensive nuclear toy called Bloody Mary that hadn't bobbed up in the ocean where it was supposed to bob up. Somebody had taken it. The question was who?

'You said Eternity,' I said.

'That's my bet,' she said. 'But everybody has their own ideas.'

'What would they want with it anyway?' I said.

'They could sell it to the highest bidder,' she said, 'Or...' then she paused and picked up the last bun, for which I had plans of my own.

'All right,' I said, 'it was mine but you can have it.'

'Thank you,' she said, and peeled away the paper. 'Or,' she said, 'they could indulge in some not very savoury nuclear blackmail.'

'Oh,' I said.

'Oh indeed,' she said.

'Can't we raid them?' I asked.

She said that would be fairly pointless. Bloody

Mary wasn't very big, compact enough to fit in a small suitcase. We wouldn't know where to begin looking. The Eternity tanker had been boarded and searched, and nothing had been found. If they had Bloody Mary they might bring it to Dublin. If they did bring it to Dublin ... then we had troubles.

'What do you do about a man with an H. bomb in his brewery?' I said, somewhat concerned at what I was getting into.

In the first place, Grace said, it wasn't exactly an H. bomb.

'Will it blow us all up if it goes off?' I said.

'Yes,' she said.

'Then it's an H. bomb,' I said.

'Letting that pass for the moment,' she said, 'you don't line up the United Nations against him, because it won't get you very far. You just hang around and wait your chance. If you're lucky you get it back ... if you're not, you pay the price he's asking.'

'Oh,' I said.

'If we're lucky,' Grace said, 'whoever has Bloody Mary won't show up here. If we're not...' she wrinkled her nose expressively.

'We...' I said.

'WE,' she said.

'Now Grace,' I said, 'you know I have my own little problems to attend to. I'm a professional person. At this very moment I'm on a commission from a most influential client. I can't possibly wait round for Bloody Mary, my life just isn't organised like that.'

'Chloe can wait,' she said, sourly.

'How did you know about Chloe?' I said.

'Never mind. But you wouldn't like Chloe to get in

49

touch with your friend Heindleighter, would you ...
knowing the way he feels about dud cheques and
Chinese elephants that aren't.'

I said she wouldn't dare put Chloe on to Heindleighter and she said she would, if she had to. Then
she said I could make a nice holiday of it, sitting
round in Dublin on a retainer from her friends. No
need to get mixed up in anything nasty unless Bloody
Mary actually put in an appearance.

'How much?' I said.

'Twenty-five pounds a week,' she said. 'Minimum
£100.'

'I didn't know you'd got friends like that,' I said,
much impressed. A hundred pounds was my sort of
money, especially as I could fill out Chloe's require-
ments while I was at it. In the remote event of Bloody
Mary turning up in Dublin I could always take to my
bed with yellow fever.

'Done,' I said.

'Good,' she said.

I smiled at her and she smiled at me, it was all most
agreeable. Thinking to make the sort of small talk
that might interest her, I told her about Eternity con-
trolling the Irish Post Office Telephone Service.

'No time for jokes,' she said.

'True,' I said.

Then I told her about my contretemps with the
telephone operator, and his concern for Eternity's
feelings.

'You've been done,' she said.

Not so, I said, into the telephone box I'd gone,
rung up in the usual way, asked to be put through
to Alice's number at M.2, and the operator had

advised me against it because it would upset Eternity.

She got up. 'Pay the bill,' she said sternly, putting on her little leather gloves.

'Charming,' I said. 'You dope my lady-friend and then you expect me to pay for your morning coffee. Mine would have been laid on at Imogen's and served at the bedside. Let me tell you I'll have to look for lodgings now, and that will cost something.'

'Pay for my coffee,' she said, 'and I'll explain all about your telephone call.'

So I paid the bill, wondering if I could get it back on the expenses from Alice. I'd come to Dublin under Chloe's steam, but it seemed to me that M.2 ought to pay up from the moment Garvey died. But Garvey, it could be argued, wasn't dead. At this my reasoning collapsed.

'Take me to the van,' Grace said, as we shouldered our way down Grafton Street. We trekked on to the van, a walk which I was getting rather used to.

'There it is,' I said, 'I know it by the sten gun in the back.'

'And your telephone box?' Grace asked.

So I pointed across the street to where the telephone box was.

Only it wasn't.

'Oh dear,' I said.

'Shall we look for it, lamb,' she said sweetly, with what I thought was unnecessary delight at my discomfort.

'I don't understand,' I said, trailing across the road after her. 'I just don't begin to understand.'

We walked solemnly up and down, and her two rabbit teeth appeared again on her lip, but otherwise

51

she made no further comment. There was certainly no telephone box in sight.

'I know,' I said. 'They must have parked the van in another street, a street with a telephone box. This can't be where I left it at all.'

'You found it quite easily on both occasions,' she said.

'All right,' I said, 'I give in. All I know is that I made a telephone call from a box directly opposite the van.'

'No you didn't,' she said.

I admitted that the evidence was in her favour, but stuck to my point. A telephone call, I insisted, on the very spot where I was standing.

'You only *think* that you did,' she said.

I looked very cross, because I was.

'You picked up the receiver,' she said. 'You dialled the operator and the operator spoke to you, is that right?'

'Yes,' I said, heavily. 'Standing in the telephone box. And the telephone box was right here where I'm standing now.'

She said that she could see that, from the marks round my feet. So I looked down at my feet and there were marks all right, making roughly a square, just where I stood. 'Thank God for something,' I said, because I'd been worried about too much excitement leading to overstrain.

'It may have looked like a telephone box,' she said. 'It may even once have been a telephone box, but it didn't belong to the post office, and it was anything but a fixture in the street.'

I must have looked a little bemused.

52

'It isn't really so extraordinary when you think about it,' she said. 'Take it the other way round. They knew when they were going to release you, and they must have had a pretty shrewd idea where you'd make for and that once you'd checked that the body had got up and walked away you would try to get in touch with your London office. For an organisation with the resources of Eternity, a telephone box, even a portable one, was no impossibility. If you hadn't gone to the van, or if you'd gone to the van and not used the phone, they'd simply have come round and taken it away again. They had nothing to lose, and everything to gain.'

'How do you mean?' I said.

'What started you thinking they really might be able to bring back the dead?' she said.

And there she had it. If they could control the G.P.O., they could control anything. But they couldn't control the G.P.O.

'It was a nice try,' Grace said.

'A very dirty trick,' I said, thinking of the shock it had been to my system. I'd almost made for the first boat back to Britain.

'Thank you for clearing that up,' I said, but Grace had already disappeared through a small wooden gate in the wall behind us. I took a deep breath and went after her, prepared for almost anything by this time. On a nearby tombstone lay the remains of someone's supper, a cold chicken, and by the wall was a snipped off coil of wire.

'The telephone exchange,' Grace said drily.

I sat down on the tomb, alongside the skeleton of the chicken.

'Don't be put out,' she said. 'It's rather an old trick, when you know your man is a stranger to the town. When you've been in the business as long as I have you'll learn to recognise these things.'

'Yes,' I said.

We went back to the van because Grace said she wanted to have a look round inside. I said I wasn't too keen on that as an idea, in case Eternity saw us.

'Nonsense,' she said. 'You're getting very timid, lamb.'

I said it was all right for her, she hadn't been given twenty-four hours to get out of town by people who just might be able to work miracles. Then I followed her across the road to the van.

She climbed into the back and I took up guard against the open door, so that nobody would see the sten gun and start asking nasty questions.

'Hurry up,' I said, as she rummaged.

'Chicken?' she said.

'Yes,' I said.

Then somebody came out of a house two doors up and stood there looking at us as if we were a circus. I smiled agreeably back. He folded his arms across a large chest and scratched his balding head, then he came wobbling forward.

'Grace,' I said urgently, 'there's a man coming,' addressing my remarks to her ski-panted behind, which was all of her that was visible from my angle.

'Then say hello,' she said.

'Good afternoon,' the large man said, putting his hand on the door of the van, and balancing himself somewhat precariously. There was something familiar about his voice, but I couldn't place it, and it began to worry me. All the bad men so far had been tiny or medium, so at least menaces were out.

'Good afternoon,' I said.

'Is that,' he said, with some authority, considering his apparent intoxication, 'is that your van?'

'No,' I said, quick witted.

'Yes,' Grace said, equally quick witted, because her presence upside down inside it would have taken some explaining, not to mention the sten gun. If I'd been apparently-dead-Garvey coming to life in the back of the van, I'd have taken the sten gun with me when I strolled away, being aware of the re-sale potential, not that a sten gun is the easiest thing in the world to carry round.

'The van belongs to the lady,' I said, craftily extricating myself.

He moved sideways to try to see past me, either to ogle her or to see the sten gun, but I wasn't having any, so I moved sideways with him. He moved back to his original position. Then it occurred to me that his movement was the direct result of the load he was carrying, and innocent of ulterior motive.

'Friend,' I said, 'you are drunk. Please go away.'

'There were people in your van,' he said, and sat down on the back of the van, thrusting me backwards against the sten, which was uncomfortable to say the least.

'What people?' I said.

'A man got out of the back,' he said.

'Describe him,' I said, and he described Garvey.

In a state of shock, I called Grace from her labours.

55

She scrambled out and came round to us, dusting her hands on her ski-pants. The large man tried to stand up, but couldn't make it.

'Friend or foe?' Grace asked.

'Witness,' I said.

With some difficulty we got him back into the house. It was small and dusty, two up and two down, green and cream wallpaper mildewed to match the curtains, a Sacred Heart in the hallway and a hip bath full of coal in the kitchen.

We set him down on the sofa.

'Empty,' Grace said, tapping the bottle on the table. This was a disaster, because after the large man's information I felt much in need of some comfort.

'Cup of tea,' I said, smiling at Grace nicely. 'A woman's place is in the home,' I said, showing her who was Lord and Master and also that I could quip bravely even when faced with the impossible.

She put the kettle on the hob, which was a piece of living history in itself. I watched full of admiration as she lifted the tea from the Yeats Memorial Tea Urn, but I wasn't admiring the tea urn, I was admiring Grace, who filled her ski-pants and sweater almost to perfection, always allowing for the bulge of the flick knife she kept strapped round her thigh. For once, even Grace seemed a little taken aback, and not without cause.

'You look very pretty today dear,' I said, thinking to chat her up, as our alcoholic friend had passed into a deep slumber beside me.

'Thank you,' she said. I waited patiently for the

return compliment, but it didn't come. She was far too busy going through the papers on the dresser.

'You shouldn't do that,' I said. 'It isn't ethical.'

'Keough,' she said.

Something went click inside me.

Maggie Keough. She was the only sizeable villain I'd met, and he was the spitting image, except that he was bald and she was a lady. The Cork accent confirmed it.

'There's a Maggie Keough mixed up in this,' I said. 'There's quite a resemblance.'

'Joe,' Grace said.

Then she started making little signs in the air over his head. I thought she'd gone funny, and then I thought she was being deadly crafty. Obviously Grace didn't think Joe Keough was as drunk as he was making out.

'I must go out and lock the van,' I said, and she gave me a congratulatory smile. We had the makings of a great team.

I went out into the hall and closed the front door noisily. Then I slipped upstairs, to see what I could see. I opened the first door I came to, and there was nothing inside at all, not a stick of furniture, not even a grate in the fireplace. On the window was a poster for a Ceilidh and a cigarette packet sat on the mantelpiece. It was empty, so I put it back.

The second room was the same. Funny, I thought, doing my Dudley, and trying to keep my feet from echoing on the bare boards. The walls were damp too, and the dust pretty thick. Obviously the place hadn't been lived in for ages.

Downstairs I went, tiptoeing past the kitchen.

where Grace was chatting Joe Keough up, and past the fishtank in the hall which I now regarded with unblushing suspicion. Somebody had set up a show-house downstairs, apparently for our benefit. I put it down provisionally to Eternity, which seemed to indicate a doubt about the allegiances of the Keoughs.

Into the front parlour, I thought, search for cryptic clues.

So I went into the front parlour and bumped into the cryptic clue, which dominated the décor. It was a large telephone box, last seen on the road outside. It looked just like the real thing, and I could understand my initial mistake. What I couldn't understand was how they'd got it into the tiny house, unless it was collapsible.

I thought I'd better take a look inside, so I walked round to the door and peered through the glass.

I could see my reflection. I smiled at me, but I didn't smile back. My nose was up against the glass, and my eyes had a glassy glitter.

So it wasn't my reflection.

I opened the door of the telephone box and the man who'd been propped up inside fell out.

'Oh,' I said.

Then I bent down to have a closer look at him.

It was Everard, the American, who had lived up to his reputation of being expendable.

CHAPTER SIX

'Grace dear,' I said, from the door, 'I wonder if you can spare me a moment?'

Grace frowned, put down her cup of tea and said something polite to Joe Keough who was sitting with his feet up on the sofa.

'You made a lot of noise,' she said, when we were out in the hall.

I said I'd just been expressing my surprise at finding a telephone box in the front room with a dead man inside it. That sort of thing, I intimated, didn't happen to everybody every day, and when it did a little consternation seemed called for. I could see from the expression on her face that she thought it all a bit old hat.

'Look,' I said pointing at the slumped form of Everard, stone cold on the bare-wooden boards.

'Do we know him?' she said, very Duchess-at-the-ball.

'As a matter of fact,' I said, 'we do.'

She said she would buy it.

So I told her he was Everard, the American I was supposed to keep tabs on for Vikdor, and about his reputation for being expendable. She said that was very nice, but who was Vikdor? I said I didn't really know but he owned a helicopter and had a vested interest in a Maggie Keough and thought I was Garvey, which seemed to me a pretty tight and comprehensive resumé of what had been a hectic incident. What's more, I said, he'd been paying Garvey to betray M.2, had this Vikdor.

'Garvey always betrays everybody,' Grace said, with an air of distaste, looking down at poor dead Everard.

'Everard was from the C.I.A. or one of those,' I said. 'American anyway. They sent him to investigate Eternity and Eternity found out.'

'How?' Grace said, but I didn't tell her. It didn't seem strictly relevant.

'You look as if you have a guilty secret,' Grace said, which I thought was very smart of her.

'Not at all,' I said.

'If you did slip up about him,' Grace said, 'I shouldn't let it worry you. My guess is that Eternity had tabs on him already.'

'What makes you think that?' I said.

'Because they seem to know their way around,' she said. 'They knew all about you, didn't they? They have a file on me. They're obviously interested in espionage people.'

Then we heard a noise next door, which might or might not have been Joe Keough moving about.

'In you go,' Grace said. 'Stay with him. I don't know why he led us here, but I'm going to capitalise on the situation.'

Oh no, I said, I was a big boy now and I expected to have things explained to me before I sat round waiting for hundreds of nasty gunmen to come bursting through the door and shooting me up. If it was a trap, I said, why should I volunteer to be the cheese?

'If you must know,' she said, 'I'm going to slip the word to Alice Alexander.'

I said I'd always understood that she had it in for Alice, not considering that the cream of Britain's secret service was good enough. She said she thought that Bloody Mary called for official intervention. Alice was accredited, she said, it would be easier for Alice.

Wait a bit, I said, none of this helps me if it is a trap.

She said I would be all right if I kept my eyes open, which seemed nothing but an empty sentiment to me. 'Be brave,' she said, which should have gone without saying.

'Give Alice my love,' I said with a reckless smile, facing up to the kitchen where cunning Joe Keough lay listening to our conversation through the bugged goldfish, ready to summon his mates to shoot me up.

'Sexy,' Grace said, and left.

Tensely I waited for the bad men to arrive, while Joe Keough faked slumber on the sofa. I whiled away my time with an unexpurgated *News of the World* which I found hidden under a cushion. Not for many a long Sunday had I enjoyed the luxury of reading the uncensored version, with all the bits about vicars left intact. I wondered if I'd missed my vocation. All those ladies in the choir at your mercy, not to mention the odd backhander from the Poor Box. Then I entered the Bathing Belle Contest, A, E, J, F,

61

B, and enjoyed Laya Raki's tummy which happened to come to hand. It seemed, and is I'm sure, a splendid tummy, deserving the highest praise.

'You from Eternity?' Joe said, from the sofa.

'No,' I said, getting ready to spring for the door.

He sat up, looking shaky.

'I'm an antique dealer,' I said. 'I'm just over here on a holiday, but things keep happening.'

'I thought you were with M.2,' he said, disconcertingly. So much for being a secret service. 'Actor and antique dealer,' I said, sticking to my guns.

'But you're not with Eternity?' he said, pressing the point.

'No,' I said.

He got to his feet and came towards me. I clenched my fists and wondered which bit of him to pummel, there was a lot to select from. He was almost uncannily like his sister Maggie. He sat down at the kitchen table, drumming his fingers on the plastic squared top.

'You know about that?' he said, nodding towards the room that contained the telephone box.

I nodded.

'They made me keep it there,' he said. 'But that thing ... that thing in the box. I didn't know he was in there, honest I didn't. I didn't know there'd be anything like that. They said it was all a joke, pretending it was a phonebox to catch somebody out. I wasn't supposed to look inside at all, only I did. Well you do, don't you, with a thing like that in the house? You want to know what it's all about.'

I said I could understand his feelings.

'I've lived here for years,' he said, which I knew to

62

be untrue, 'I've never had no trouble, not till Maggie came.'

'Maggie?' I said, as if I didn't know.

'My sister,' he said. 'Twins, we were. Now I don't know ... can't understand what she does to get it all.'

'All what?' I said.

'All that money,' he said.

Then he got up and walked across to the kitchen door, opening it to reveal a little yard at the back. 'Got to go out the back,' he said, and turned to go through it.

There was a bang, and he gave a grunt, and staggered forward, then another shot followed, and he fell over something out of my view. A bullet shattered the bottle of Lourdes Water that hung on the wall opposite the door.

I didn't stop to think about who was doing the shooting. I was down on the floor and under the sofa in double quick time. There is a moral in the story, which is always survey your ground before people start shooting at you, just in case they miss.

Somebody evil had shot Joe Keough. If it was a trap, he'd been included in the bait, perhaps unknowingly. I peered cautiously out. There was a window by the table, looking out over the yard, but I couldn't see through it because of my peculiar cramped position under the sofa.

The next thing was a clatter in the yard, somebody arriving clumsily from the wall where the assassin must have crouched with his rifle.

'You get him Sam?' somebody said.

I recognised both voice and name. It was Ana-

63

stasia's Antiques all over again, except that this time there were two corpses on the premises instead of one and I was under Joe Keough's sofa instead of up on the top of Garvey's four-poster. A tiny problem was the question of who hired Small Sam and his unseen mate to go round hitting people with ice-picks and shooting them in their backyards, but I didn't stop to think about it, not just then. Survival was the immediate problem.

The window rose and a black-gloved hand groped through the space, disturbing a plastic model of Arkle, with Pat up. Then a tin rolled across the table, taking the Yeats Memorial Tea Urn with it.

There followed a frantic commotion in the yard. 'Door won't open,' Small Sam said, probably not able to reach the bolt. Then there was a crash, which must have been his mate attacking the door, and getting through it unceremoniously.

I wasn't sorry to hear them go.

I didn't want to make any dramatic move, in case it was the wrong one. My position didn't help contemplation either, because I was wedged up against a pussycat nightie-case, with a broken spring from the sofa pressing down on my spine.

I put my muddled thinking down to these distractions, because without them I would undoubtedly have realised that the tin was a bomb right away.

As it was, I looked at it nestling against the leg of the sofa where it had come to a stop and I thought to myself: 'That's not a tin, that's a bomb, probably.'

A *bomb*.

I kicked it hard, almost taking the sofa with me. It started to fizz. I rolled clear of the sofa and made a dive at the door. The bomb went off with a great crash, so that the blast picked me up and hurled me down the hall past the Sacred Heart, finishing the job off by smashing me against the front door, which I hit with a dirty great thud.

My arm was all bloody. I lay there clutching the remains of a hallstand which had appeared from I know not where, and watching a goldfish splutter its life away on the mat, thinking how glad I was that I was indestructible, because anybody else would have been blown to pieces. Then I started checking the pieces, just to make sure that I hadn't been. All of them were in place, but my jacket was ripped open from the shoulder, and my arm was numb. Obviously a peasant-type bomb, because the fizzing ones went out with the Great War.

I stood up and opened the front door, what was left of it. I was very groggy indeed but conscious enough to know that I couldn't afford to stay there waiting for Grace to come and ask me what had happened. There were too many corpses around, the sort of thing even a peasant republic won't tolerate.

I propped myself against the van for a moment, and something else exploded in the house behind me, which must have been the gas. There was a lot of smoke pouring out through the open door, and I realised in a vague way that the two corpses weren't going to be found after all, or at least not until they'd been toasted.

'What's on?' a man said, standing looking at my blood and tatters. 'Had a bit of trouble?'

Doors were banging open and people popping out

of their houses to have a look. I shouldered my way past the man and the rest of them gave way before me, showing proper respect for the wounded. Then I saw a uniform coming and stood quite still as it passed me, on the trot. My feet weighed like concrete bricks and there was a lot wrong with my arm, so that I found it difficult to concentrate on walking at all.

The next thing I remember is lying against a wall tracing the cracks in blue painted concrete and trying to hold myself upright by propping my leg against it. It seemed to be very dark and I remember thinking how curious it was, the time being about mid-day. Then the wall with the cracks started to waver before my eyes and I thought, no going unconscious, because you'll get caught.

So I pushed myself along the wall, bouncing off and bumping back on. I put my hand in a puddle of water, and it hurt like hell and I realised I was lying on the ground, though I didn't know how I'd got there.

I registered that someone was pulling at my arms, trying to lift me up.

Somebody said, 'Are you all right, chum?'

'Maggie Keough,' I said, recognising her steel-tipped shoes.

'That's a terrible cut you have, Garvey,' she said.

'I could use some of your pot,' I said, conscious that my voice seemed to come from a very, very long way off. We stumbled through a doorway, and I remember thinking how very muscular she was. She shoved me into a dark place and put me down on something that was harsh and cold against my leg. I remember feeling cross because I realised that something had ripped the leg of my nice trousers, the Donegal tweed ones that Imogen gave me. It was too bad.

Maggie Keough went away, closing a door on me and shutting out the light. Then I heard a bolt slip home. I wasn't falling for that, even if she was Vikdor's lady. So I tried to get up, but I slipped and fell against the door. I found myself lying on a stone floor with my head against a stack of turf brickettes, without the strength to go on trying.

I looked up and saw a lavatory cistern covered in rust. There was a chain hanging down from it, with a bit of string added and I thought, if somebody pulled that, I'd just go down the pan, and that would be the end of it all, wouldn't it?

Later, it must have been very much later, although I had no real conception of the time involved, I wakened up.

I was lying propped against the turf bricks but someone had put a woman's fur coat and an army blanket over me, which seemed to mean that the natives were friendly. I tried to move my arm and remembered about it all in the same split second, because it hurt so badly. There was a great thick bandage wrapped round it, the remnant of a sheet, and below the bandage my wrist had swollen up like a pineapple.

Oh dear, I thought.

I moved my other arm to see if it worked, and it did, although there was some elastoplast on my hand which indicated cuts. My legs were stiff and sore, but there were no breakages.

A celebration seemed to be in order. It isn't every day that you get blown up and live to tell the tale, not as thoroughly close-range blown up as I'd been. It ought to have been worth a medal, except that they don't give medals to secret agents. At least they wouldn't give me one, because Bandy Alice would never entertain the idea.

Get up, I thought, and so I got up.

I tried the door, and it opened. This was strange because my last memory was Maggie Keough locking it behind her. I thought about it a bit and arrived at a possible solution, which was a happy one. She had locked it so that no policemen who might be looking for me could get in. By now they'd have given up the idea, so she'd opened it again. Maggie was apparently on my side.

I had to qualify that at once. She was on Vikdor's side and Vikdor was on the side of the real Garvey. If they once realised that the real Garvey had been dead from the outset, I would be in trouble ... for the sake of simplicity I dismissed the impostor Garvey at Eternity from my mind, he couldn't be a factor, because if he was it meant they could bring people back from the dead. Then I found I wasn't as sure about that as I had been.

I found a green door and knocked on it. A man in a white coat answered.

'Mr. Garvey,' he said. 'Do come in. We didn't want to move you, not till we had everything ready.'

I followed him into a kitchen the double of Joe Keough's, though without Arkle and Pat and the Yeats Memorial Urn.

'If you'll just sit there Mr. Garvey,' he said, 'we'll

give you a little shot of something to put you out.'

I sat, but I said I'd just come back from being out, and was it absolutely necessary to start all over again?

He said I wasn't to worry about it. Then he stuck a syringe into my arm and I went to sleep, feeling too weak to argue about it.

Later, much later, I came to momentarily.

'Where am I?' I asked a small man in overalls and a mask.

'You're in an aeroplane crossing over the Eastern zone,' he said, gently.

I smiled, to show my appreciation. They call it cheer therapy. 'No, but really,' I said, at my drowsiest, but still feeling I ought to take an interest. 'I'd like to know where to send the wreath.'

He took the syringe out of my arm and wiped it.

'Gorteburg,' he said.

Somehow it didn't sound like an Irish name.

CHAPTER SEVEN

I've always considered myself a Hardy man, having a special soft spot for the assassin kiddy Little Father Time who hung all nice Jude's babes on the back of the door because there were too many of them. It was a good thing to do because they hadn't much to contribute to the plot and would have been a terrible burden on the ratepayers. I thought Hardy hit on the ideal way to get rid of them, but, even for an enthusiast, you can have too much of Thomas.

So I rang the little bell at the bedhead and waited, impatiently tapping the dazzling white sheets with my sling.

The bearded nurse came striding in, her white uniform all crisp and crackling. I didn't like her very much, but her beard lent an air of mystery.

I told her exactly what I thought about being kept penned up in a private room I-knew-not-where with only the Collected Thomas to keep me company, and woggy editions at that, with bad spines and inferior print. I said I had business to be about, wagging my sling at her to show I could wag it now. All healed up, I said, even my stitches had stopped itching.

The bearded nurse said she would get me a sedative.

'That,' I said, 'is not good enough. I am a British Citizen. I know all about Irish hospitals and no

National Health. You are out to get at my capital. I demand to see someone in charge.' Actually the joke was on them, because I hadn't any capital and had already made a considerable hole in Chloe's market money before disaster overtook me.

'This is not possible,' she said. She was on the large side for a lady and very well preserved, apart from her little beard, which wasn't her fault, I suppose, but one of nature's quips.

'If you don't fetch someone in authority at once, I shall get up out of this bed and walk out,' I said. 'Then your bill will never get paid.'

'You must rest,' she said, kindly but firmly.

Obviously I wasn't getting anywhere. She stood there at the foot of the bed looking at me over my medical chart. I'd already tried to read it, but I couldn't, because it was in some sort of code.

Try charm, I thought.

'What is your name?' I asked, with a devilish glitter in my eye which I thought she might appreciate. I knew and she knew that I couldn't run away through the streets of Dublin in my pyjamas, Dublin not being Earls Court, where I would have chanced it, but she was bound to admire my spirit.

'Nana,' she said, flashing yellow teeth at me. So much for dark-eyed, soft-voiced colleens rushing to my every need. I grudged every penny I'd spent on their Hospital Sweepstakes in the past.

'What a pretty name,' I said, wondering if I could try her with Zola or whether it was safer to stick to Peter Pan and Wendy, though on second appraisal I decided that she wasn't a literary type, it would have been bread on the waters.

'Well Nana,' I said, 'perhaps you can tell me where I am, as a very special favour?'

'This is not possible,' she said, gravely.

'Now listen, Nana,' I said, somewhat more severely. 'When I tell the Mother Superior about you there will be trouble.' I thought that a pretty shrewd blow because it was an Irish hospital and there was bound to be a Mother Superior somewhere in the offing.

'I do not comprehend you,' she said, and turned on her heel.

'Just you come back here, peasant,' I called, as she strode through the door, but she stayed gone. I sat up in bed feeling very cross. Nana with the beard was the only living person I'd seen since coming to. My arm was still a little stiff and my memory of what had happened a little blurred, but apart from that I was sound in wind and limb and much concerned about Grace, Alice Alexander and Chloe's Irish knick-knacks, which were, after all, a source of income not to be despised.

Out of bed and have a pad round, I thought.

I got out and stood on the cold stone floor, which was torture, as they didn't rise to bedsocks. Neither did they rise to decent pyjamas, so that I had to hold the tops across my chest when Nana was there, in case she got excited. The pyjamas weren't the only antiques either, for the shutters on the windows had seen better days, as also had the little oil lamp which operated with a lovely little string pull and a brass ring. Apart from the lamp there was nothing in the room but a small black chair and the bed. Paint of an institutional grey covered the walls, which were very thick, to judge by the window, so that the place had something of the appearance of a mediaeval bed-sitter.

I padded across to the door and stuck my head out, into a long corridor paved with large grey stone slabs. There was a door a few yards away and I tried it, thinking that it might be a clothes closet, but it was locked.

I went back to my bed and sat on the end, thinking. No strip lighting, no rubberised floors, no little trolleys with silver cans and forceps, no arrows with ward numbers, no black-eyed colleens, not even a nun. My only evidence was bearded Nana and she re-enforced the conclusion that I was not in a hospital after all.

Given that, I could be anywhere, almost. There was a bit in my mind which might or might not have been a dream about being in an aeroplane over Gorteburg. If it wasn't a dream, Gorteburg was where I was.

But where was Gorteburg?

Somebody coughed. I looked up, and standing in the doorway was Vikdor, still wearing his leather coat.

'My dear Garvey,' he said. 'I'm so glad to learn that you are making a recovery. We were most distressed to learn that you had been injured.'

'So was I,' I said.

He sat down on the plastic chair, making a nonsense of it with his size.

'Uncomfortable things,' he said. 'But we have to put up with a little discomfort, things being as they are in this part of the world. I hope you are being well looked after.'

I said bearded Nana was a gem.

'Maggie Keough was most upset,' he said. 'She seemed to hold herself in some degree responsible for your injuries. I hope you will forgive her.'

'Of course,' I said, then I asked how she was taking the news about her brother.

'Her brother?' Vikdor said.

'He's dead,' I said, 'somebody shot him.'

Vikdor laughed. 'There must be some mistake,' he said. 'Maggie has no brother.'

'I think you are mistaken,' I said. Then I told him I thought Maggie was too friendly with Eternity.

'I should hope so,' he said.

'Oh,' I said.

'Maggie is a first-rate operator,' he said.

'Trustworthy?'

He smiled. 'Who is trustworthy in our business? She is well paid, very well paid.'

There seemed a possibility that I too would be very well paid, plus compensation for getting blown up, if I could only keep him thinking I was Garvey till we got to the bank.

'That's nice to know,' I said.

'Quite,' he said, allowing a bland smile to close the subject. 'If you feel fit for it, there is someone I would like you to meet, before we have our little discussion.'

'Oh?' I said.

'You remember a man named Lefle?' he said.

Well, did I? It might or might not be a test question. Lefle could be somebody I *had* to know, like my daddy. Garvey-whose-real-name-was-Lebnowitz might have had all shapes and sizes of nearest and dearest I'd never heard about. The sum total of my information

74

was the bit about being the distant cousin of a
Russian count. What if this man Lefle denounced me
as an imposter?

'Lefle,' I said, playing for time, my mind resolutely
refusing to jump without looking first.

'He worked for your uncle in Paris,' Vikdor said.

'My uncle in Paris,' I said, taking it all in, and
thinking that this repeating was a great game. In no
time at all I would have enough on Garvey to live the
part for life.

'He's coming to see you,' Vikdor said. 'Said he
wanted a private chat, before we moved on to the
main issue.'

'Is that wise?' I said. 'I feel a little weak.'

'Your old friend will cheer you,' Vikdor said,
inscrutably. 'I am sure you will have a happy talk.'

Panic.

'When?' I asked.

'Now,' he said.

My Anastasia bit, like Ingrid in that nice film,
except that Ingrid had rehearsal money and a kind of
a sort of a script and nobody was going to take her out
into the woods and shoot her if she fluffed her lines.
The springing of Garvey's uncle's old retainer on me
was a decidedly unpleasant turn-up, making me
doubt Vikdor's faith in my identity.

They dressed me up in a brown serge suit of un-
inspired cut and a chunky roll-neck sweater and led
me along a corridor and down some steps to a little
egg-yellow room with a 1958 Pepsi Cola calendar on
the wall, where they abandoned me. Not only did
they abandon me, they locked the door behind me,

leaving me to brood on the Pepsi girl and how she'd found her way there. Bearded Nana and Vikdor seemed very happy together, maybe they had something running for them. Either she was kinky for leather coats or he was kinky for little beards.

There was a nice desk in the room, which I went rapidly through, not omitting the secret door with the catch in the rose pattern at the back. It yielded a Mars Bar wrapper, presumably from the same source as the Pepsi lady, but no gun to shoot my way out with or other relevant equipment, such as a little pill to take before they put the screws on. All I found was a guide book to Peking in an unintelligible language. I could tell it was Peking because of the pictures, but it didn't help me. So I gave up looking for help and started looking for the microphone, which would be covering the reunion with my uncle's old retainer. It wasn't behind the Pepsi lady or in the keyhole, but clamped securely to the underside of the seat I was supposed to be sitting in. It was very big, almost egg-sized, which didn't say much for their technology, whatever flag they flew.

Cut the wires, I thought.

But I didn't cut the wires, partly because I had no wire-cutters and partly because I knew a trick worth two of that from the weekend training course at Southsea I talked Alice into letting me attend. The idea was that when Lefle arrived I would sit tight and grip the side of the chair, then pat my fingers up and down against the mike when we started talking. It would give them earache, and no information.

It did occur to me that if they were being deadly cunning they would have put that one in as a blind and another one the size of a pin head would be some-where where I'd never find it. I didn't bother looking for that one, taking their talent as read.

'Alexi,' the guttural voice said, full of affection.

'Old friend,' I said because it seemed a reasonably safe thing to say, keeping my head firmly down and my chin tucked in.

'Let me look at you,' he cried. Well, there wasn't much I could do about it, put that way. So I looked up at him and smiled appealingly, trying to look like the distant cousin of a Russian aristocrat gone raffish.

He kissed me on both cheeks, which I thought was a pretty disgusting thing, but I didn't dare say so. He was a scruffy little man, about up to my shoulder. He wore a wine coloured polo-neck sweater and jeans, and his hair was dyed a violent yellow, what there was of it. I didn't know what to think. If I played up to him and he was a grocer's boy from Leningrad they had me and if I denied him and he was genuine they had me just as clearly. Then I decided that 'old friend' had committed me.

'It is so good to see you after all this time,' I said and, just to cover my bets, 'I can scarcely believe it is you, the years have indeed changed us.' Though I say it myself, I thought that was a pretty deft switch.

'I would have known you anywhere, Alexi,' he said, with passionate feeling. He gripped my jacket tightly, overcome by his emotion. I disengaged his sweaty hand with some difficulty, feeling a bit of a cad for trading on his affections and defective memory.

He sat down opposite me and said something in Wog-talk.

'Stop,' I said, 'it hurts too much to speak the old tongue.'

He nodded sympathetically. I wondered what the hell he'd said, and hoped it wasn't important.

'Do you remember the cherry trees?' he asked.

'Yes,' I said, hopefully.

'Then I should forget them,' he said. 'There were no cherry trees.'

'Oh,' I said.

'Alice sent me,' he said. 'If you will continue tapping on that microphone perhaps we may enjoy a little private conversation.'

That evening we had dinner by candle-light, amid the remains of what had once been considerable splendour. Now the shutters were rudely bared and the chandeliers had been taken away; philistine wogs had looted the silver plate. Something of the past remained in the beautiful ceiling and the carving by the mantelpiece, though not in our conversation, which was mundane, when it wasn't nasty. I wish I could have taken it all home with me and put on Imperial gear and gone around in a sleigh calling people serf.

We were all slightly on edge. Lefle and I talked like the old buddies we weren't while Vikdor and Nana obviously wanted to get back to doing whatever they'd been doing before we turned up.

We sat there and sipped in the light of a lovely log fire until Vikdor, with elaborate show, produced a handy-sized tape recorder and set it on the coffee table before us.

'Are we all ready?' he said, with an air of ceremony.

78

'Let us have another drink or two first,' I said.

So we did, whilst Vikdor checked the batteries. It had to run on batteries because our lovely house had no electricity. For once I felt on top of the world and in control of the situation. I was in-the-know, going-to-be-on-the-winning-side. Lefle was on my side because he knew who I really was, Lefle being present as the official representative of M.2. Vikdor was on my side too, because he didn't know who I was. We were having a top-level conference and I held all the cards. As I say, I was very happy about it, and about the vodka.

'Gentlemen, your attention,' Vikdor said, and then he twiddled the little knob.

Memorandum of meeting between Major Vikdor, Alexi Lebnowitz and Colonel Lefle held at Gorteburg, March 17, 1967.

To discuss the organisation known as Eternity Brewers of Dublin.

Finding. We are in agreement that a certain course be adopted, the cost of which to be borne equally between the two services under conditions as recognised in the Kramer Symposium, 1949.

The Operation to be controlled by Colonel Lefle of British Intelligence with the assistance of Alexi Lebnowitz of the division.

The Objective to be an investigation of the organisation known as Eternity Brewers of Dublin.

The Priority of the operation to be *immediate*.

> *Authorisation*
> For C.B.D. .... Major Vikdor
> For M.2 ... Colonel A. A. Lefle.

CHAPTER EIGHT

It was good to breathe British air again, even if it was contaminated. I felt a little tense, which I suppose was understandable, being about to commence the joint operation which was to bring Eternity to its lush knees.

Cool down, I commanded myself, as the rain beat down upon me, mingling with the spring snow which has suddenly become a feature of our lives.

Bracknell, said the roadsigns, but it was no longer the Bracknell of my youth, a Bracknell of forest walks and lovely wooden houses full of yeomen and wood-cutters. Now it was a new town, all palefaces and prams, the misbegotten offspring of planned growth. Let them eat supermarket cake, I cried, waiting for the Greenline to London and destiny.

It was late, but it did come, which is as much as you can expect these days, and stopped, which put it above average. So I got in and took my place with the plebs. Then I sat there thinking about things, which weren't too bad. M.2 were collaborating with Vikdor, who thought I was working for him, but I wasn't. M.2 had decided to let Vikdor go on thinking I was on his side, in case I came in handy. I thought this a very nice arrangement, but unfortunately no one had yet got round to paying me. I had reason to believe that Garvey's money would be paid into some secret Swiss account by Vikdor, but I could hardly ask Vikdor which one, because I was supposed to know the answer already. Grace was also paying me a substantial sum, but this was theoretical. I had yet to see the colour of her money.

Officially M.2 had joined forces with the Wogs to break Eternity, an organisation of such menace that they didn't even bother to shoot the agents who were sent against them. They picked them up, patted them on the head, and sent them back whence they came. Unofficially we were all out for Bloody Mary. Eternity could go on playing their little fiddle till the cows came home, just so long as it didn't threaten the rest of us with a nuclear holocaust, all three of my briefs said so.

What Eternity probably didn't have, according to our calculations, was the sort of nuclear expert they would need to make Bloody Mary effective. Given that they had Bloody Mary they'd find someone to work it for them sooner or later ... so we decided to find their expert for them. The right sort of expert sent off running in the right direction at the right time was called for.

That was Lefle's side of the operation. Mine was to organise the publicity to bait the trap. Desperate measures were called for, and they knew their man. With great secrecy I was delivered back to Bracknell while Lefle's side of things was arranged with the appropriate Ministries, who didn't see it all our way, by any means. I wasn't to be seen, they said. So I sat with Basil and Doris watching 'Double Your Money' till I was cross-eyed, eating food unfit for Britons, like tapioca and runner beans. The night the weatherman predicted a cyclone over Southern Ireland I went upstairs and packed my gun.

The bus roared into Victoria and I crossed over to the coach station to chalk up the first item on what I'd privately decided was going to be a formidable list of expenses. Vikdor was paying, so even Alice couldn't object, in fact spending Vikdor's money was doing Alice a favour.

Fried egg and sausage, I ordered, deciding that I needed a nice nourishing meal to keep me going through the tough dealing to come, none of your ravioli.

The lady gave me half a sausage and a cold fried egg, stuck in the split of a stale bun.

'This is not what I ordered,' I said, crossly.

'The toasted bun,' she said, 'is thrown in free.'

I prodded the bun. 'I should think it would be,' I said, and left in a huff.

My appointment was for nine-thirty, and I took my time about getting there, but even then I was too early, so I strolled across Chelsea Bridge to the coffee stall which, being-of-the-people and not part of an empire, gave me nice filling rolls and hot tea for my money ... or rather, for Vikdor's money.

I propped myself up against the parapet of the bridge and enjoyed a nostalgic moment watching the lights of Battersea on the river and remembering the Dome of Discovery and other delights from the good old days when our lion was a lion. Back in '51 we had the Wogs at our mercy and Elizabeth Taylor was still a Briton, but now things have gone to pot. Even

Vanessa took off her vest on the big screen and disgraced herself, I wonder she can look Sir Michael in the face. Buy-a-bra-for-Britain, I'd tell her, if I was her daddy. Actually I rather fancied Vanessa before she let us down, but now I've gone back to Anna Neagle.

Nine-thirty came and went, and no sign of my man, even our criminal classes are slipping. I was a bit nervous about meeting him, not being used to mixing with the lower-orders, but it had to be.

I finished my tea and got out my small gun, to have a look at it. It was loaded, which was only theoretically nice, as I wasn't clear how it worked and practising in Bracknell hadn't seemed a very good idea, because of noise. I was likely to do more harm than good with it, with the off-chance that I would shoot someone who didn't deserve it. Feeling very virtuous and self-sacrificing I took out the bullets and dropped them into the Thames; it might have gone off in my pocket and done me an injury.

A lady went past, wheeling a pram. She looked at me and smiled enigmatically. Grace, I thought, but it wasn't. I felt bad about Grace, who was probably strewing flowers on Joe Keough's house and saying soliloquies, thinking that I was with the angels. It would be a bit of a blow to her, especially as my being probably dead was all her fault. Later she was going to be delighted when she found out I was alive, which was a very pleasing prospect.

A large man beckoned to me, standing at the side of the coffee stall. He was hairy and unpleasant looking, which didn't surprise me, having read his file, which we'd had away from Criminal Records. This was no cultured Mr. Big, cigar-smoking and diamond-flashing; this was William Talbot of Shepherd's Bush, with eleven convictions for things I didn't think people did any more.

'I think you wanted a word?' he said.

'Talbot?' I said, looking at his heavily bandaged hand. Bullet wound, was my thought. Of course it might have been any sort of wound, but I was a little over excited.

'You'll be Garvey?' he said.

'Yes,' I said, and invited him to have a cup of tea on the expenses. We collected a fresh cup apiece and went to lean conspiratorially on the bridge parapet.

'Seem to know you from somewhere,' he said. 'Funny.'

'You must be mistaken,' I said, hopefully.

'Haven't I seen you at the market,' he said. 'Camden Passage?'

'Not me,' I said.

'You had a mucky old stall,' he said. 'You sold that seventeenth-century Portuguese box for fifteen bob, didn't you?'

'No,' I said. They always remember your mistakes. Nobody ever says how wonderful I was with the stuffed bird or the barrel-organ, but the Portuguese box keeps cropping up.

'Oh yes, you did,' he said. 'Fifteen bob. We all had a laugh.'

'What's it to you?' I asked, on the good old principle about taking the offensive.

'Only that your name isn't Garvey,' he said. 'Hobley or Mobley or something like that, but not Garvey.'

84

'You must be confusing me with someone else,' I said, acutely uncomfortable. It was unforgivable that my past should dent the image, just when I had my hands on glory as the man in charge of stage two of our operation. If William Talbot went around announcing I was Hobley or Mobley and talking about the Portuguese box it couldn't be long before someone told him I was me. I didn't want the name of Otley mixed up in it for very obvious reasons, not unconnected with Leather Vikdor and potentially vicious Maggie Keough.

'Could be,' he said, without trying to sound as if he was convinced of it for a minute.

'You've got things ready?' I said.

'Not quite,' he said.

'Why not?'

'We want more money,' he said, blandly.

'You're not worth it,' I said. 'We've looked you up. We know the rate for the job. You're getting that and more, because we want it to go smoothly.'

He said something about everything costing more these days, then put his cup down with a rattle. 'More money ... or some information.'

I gave a taciturn chuckle. 'You must be joking,' I said, 'there's a freeze on, remember.'

He turned back to the river. 'Nice night,' he said, reflectively, then; 'Your name isn't Garvey, it's Otley. Gerald Arthur Otley. You are a tatty little dealer and you haven't got a quid to your name, let alone the price for this job. I know you're a front, and I'd feel happier if I knew who you're fronting for.'

'I don't understand,' I said, trying to sound offended.

'You can increase your cut,' he said. 'Your boss needn't know.'

Well, if he wanted to be smart, two could play. There was no reason why I shouldn't sell him up the river if I could do it without damaging the cause.

'By how much?' I asked.

'Ten per cent of what we get,' he said.

It was quite clever, but once he knew where the money was coming from there was nothing to stop him cutting me out of the operation and spoiling my reputation at the same time.

'No,' I said. 'I want cash now.'

To my immense surprise and gratification he took a wad of notes out of his coat pocket and peeled off ten fivers. 'Well?' he said.

'People called Eternity,' I said, quick as a flash. 'Dublin boys.'

'Oh,' he said, 'I.R.A.?'

'That's it,' I said. 'One of their jobs.'

That seemed to make him very happy, and didn't seem to do any harm to me and mine, being probably the only piece of Ireland's civilisation he'd been told about, which made him a spiritual Black-and-Tan. We spent another ten minutes on the arrangements for the morning and then wished each other a cheery goodnight.

I felt very superior and sophisticated on my stroll back towards Earls Court, because the I.R.A. was just the smokescreen the situation called for if anything went wrong in the heat of the moment. I was longing to tell Alice, but I couldn't, because I wasn't supposed to know Alice. I was the tool of a great power, and in twenty-four hours the result of my enterprise would be in big black headlines all over Britain, and Colonel Lefle would be risking his neck while I collected the kudos.

I looked forward to getting back to my little room in Earls Court, last seen months before, and spending a happy night being Otley, laughing blithely in the face of all the bills I'd gone to Dublin to get away from.

As it happened, the night turned out quite differently.

The first surprise came when I reached the church in Redcliffe Square and turned to cross the road towards the house which contains my little home, hidden high up in the roofbeams in order to be nearer God. There is ten by eight of it, and me, and a bed, and a gas ring, so that even a small guest is overcrowding.

A big grey car was standing by the kerb, one of the anonymous ones M.2 use, bought second hand at great expense and identifiable by the bullet-proof glass and the furtive looking drivers. This was not in the programme. I was forbidden territory to M.2 operatives, because of pretending to be Garvey for Vikdor's benefit.

I walked slowly past the car. The driver sat up, looked at the photograph in the dossier beside her, and stuck her head out of the window.

'Otley,' she said, sounding very charming, and not at all furtive. Obviously she represented a break with tradition. Just at that moment I didn't feel as pleased about it as I might otherwise have been, because she was risking my neck.

87

Don't argue in the street, I thought, this being axiomatic in espionage.

I strode back to the car and clambered in, needing to unleash my anger and give M.2 a piece of my mind, via its sweet-voiced representative.

'Don't you know anything?' I snapped. 'You mustn't go shouting my name like that in public. There are people who might be watching, out to get me. I'm supposed to be incognito, or worse.'

'Miss Alexander wants to speak with you,' she said, bearing up bravely under my ruthless denunciation. 'Something important has come up.'

'Oh yes?' I said, trying to intimate as much disapproval of this irregular procedure as I could muster. 'May I see your authority please?'

I find it pays to make them go through the ropes, keeps them up to scratch. Most of M.2's minions have a tendency to be superior and unpleasant when they get the chance, being jealous of agents in the field, who get all the ladies. At least that's the theory. It hadn't worked out for me properly, but I remained full of hope. It couldn't be what was wrong this time of course, because this one was obviously a lady.

In fact, she was a delicious lady, as she revealed when she switched on the car light to show me the card.

'Perhaps,' I said, gazing recklessly into her green eyes, 'perhaps I should sit up in the front with you. It would be more cosy that way, especially if we have a long way to go.'

'If you wish,' she said, giving me the lush lip and allowing her golden curls to flounce around her. Life looked swiftly up, and smiled. I'm sure Alice wouldn't have sent her along if she'd thought about it, Alice being exceptionally and unreasonably mean about these things when it comes round to my turn.

'My name,' I said, just to impress it on her memory, 'is Gerald, but you may call me Gerry.'

'And my name is Miss Clews,' she said. 'You may call me Miss Clews.'

'It will be a pleasure,' I said, nothing daunted.

And it was. It was even a pleasure to sit there looking at her. The uniform jacket, blouse and skirt worked wonders on her, where they would have reduced another lady to one of M.2's furtives.

'Surely,' I said, 'a girl like you is wasted in a job like this, Miss Clews? You should be in television, or on the stage.'

'And you have friends who could put me there,' she said, as if she'd seen it coming.

'As a matter of fact I am rather influential,' I said. 'I have some connections who might well be interested, if we made the right approach.' It was just about true, though none of them had done me much good. But then I wasn't Miss Clews. I had only talent, which she didn't need.

'We could be a great team,' she said. 'All I need is a manager.'

Don't be like that Miss Clews,' I said. 'I'm thinking of you, truly I am.'

'No doubt,' she said, as if she didn't fancy it. Then she said we could talk about it when we got to Cambridge.

'Why Cambridge, Miss Clews?' I asked, trying not to sound too happy.

89

'Because that's where we're going,' she said, with infinite sweetness, and put my hand back on my knee.

We got on very well, though I say it myself. Masculine appeal is masculine appeal, an incalculable something that some people have and some people haven't, poor things. I am one of the haves.

Sylvia told me.

As it transpired we were a little early reaching Cambridge, where, Sylvia informed me, Alice Alexander was attending a Security Conference at Magdalene. It seemed a funny place to hold a Security Conference but with Sylvia looking at me like that I was in no mood to prevaricate.

With the gorgeous moon in the sky high above us we sat in the back seat of the official car and talked about What It Is Like To Be A Secret Agent. Sylvia was awfully good at listening. I said it was Mostly Routine. I said Brute Strength didn't come into it. The modern spy was a Technologist, his weapons Courage and Tenacity, backed by Know-How. I thought it was quite impressive, and Sylvia seemed to think so too.

Straightening my tie for me with her long sensuous fingers, Sylvia said that the back of the car was getting stuffy and we should go for a walk.

I said what about going round to Magdalene to look in on Alice and the top-brass, not very enthusiastically.

She said that there was plenty of time to spare, and we ought to get to know each other better.

Great.

So we strolled by the moonlit Cam. At least I told Sylvia that it was the Cam, and there was nobody around to contradict me, so I stuck to it. The pale moon shone on her golden hair and her beautiful green eyes gazed smokily into mine, and I mean smokily.

'The night,' I told her, 'is filled with a strange sensuality.' She seemed to agree. We sat on a bank and I told her what it was like to be in charge of an inter-service operation and that Death walked in my Shadow. She didn't look very impressed. In fact she straightened her skirt and expressed her disbelief, bringing me rudely back to earth.

'You are a reserve operator,' she said. 'This sounds like a job for someone much more important.'

I said I'd been on the spot when the call came, in this case the ice-pick in Garvey's chest. Fate had dealt me greatness.

She looked at me with a new respect.

'And M.2 are combining with V . . .'

'Don't,' I snapped. 'Don't speak that name.'

So she didn't. She just looked suitably impressed while I did my brave-and-troubled to her worried-little-woman.

'And you are in charge of the entire operation?' she said, with awe.

'In a manner of speaking,' I said. Well I was in charge of half of it, and taking awful risks. It didn't seem unfair to take my tiny share of the perks that were going, especially when the perks took the form of Sylvia Clews of M.2 who knew the Official Secrets Act as well as I did. It had not previously occurred to me that we had sultry seductive ladies on our side; I'd been waiting for the enemy to show their hand for ages.

We walked a little further along the dusky banks and she suggested a passionate midnight swim. At least she suggested the midnight swim, and I assumed that passion would follow as night follows day. My bit of the swimming wasn't going to last long because of the early April snow, among other things, but I could see it was just a chance for her to get at me, and I thought it charitable to let her have her way.

'Let's go in here,' she said, as we paused in the shade of a large bush.

'I have no costume,' I said, naïvely, being good at that bit although really a ruthless dilettante.

She let the saucy angle of her eyebrow indicate that with spy-people like us no costume was *the* costume. I took it like a hero who'd been expecting it.

'Be quick,' she gasped, and we parted hands and retreated behind adjacent bushes for sake of a convention which seemed a little empty in the circumstances.

This, I reflected breathlessly, was the life. I draped my suede trousers over the side of a bush and ran a casual comb through my old gold locks and, eager for action, hopped lightly over a large briar and out on to the river bank.

The water glinted in the moonlight, looking horribly cold. I tried to remind myself that it was only a means to an end. I didn't have to go in, I only had to look as if I might have if we hadn't been sidetracked before we got that far. It was all an elaborate farce so that she could conceal the real depth of her animal instincts from herself.

I dipped my toe in, just to be prepared for the worst. It confirmed my suspicions. No swimming, I thought, no swimming whatsoever.

'Come on,' I called softly to her bush. 'The water is lovely and warm.'

Silence, bleak and breezy.

An unworthy suspicion began to form in my mind, but I promptly rejected it. Not nice Sylvia.

I hopped up and down, very conscious of being in my underpants by the Cam at midnight, all ready to not take a midnight swim. It would be all right in a moment, I supposed hopefully.

But a moment passed, and another.

Where was my Sylvia?

Gone.

'Sylvia?' I cried softly, again in the general direction of her bush, where she'd gone to shed her dull uniform to reveal lacy fripperies of which I dared not think. It seemed almost unethical for her to have had second thoughts and gone back to the car after all the material I'd wasted on her. All right, I thought grimly, if that's the way you want it. Glamour girls are all the same, frightened of real men. I have a golden rule; I prefer ladies who prefer me. Sylvia Clews had appeared to qualify, but we all make mistakes. So long as she didn't complain about me to Alice I had nothing to fear.

A torch went on, catching me in its beam.

'Sylvia?' I called, although it was rather a long way off.

The torchbearer came forward down the path to me. The shape looked a bit big for Sylvia, and I somehow sensed menace.

'You're dazzling me,' I said. 'What are you trying to do, get me arrested for indecency?'

The beam wavered.

'Who the hell is that?' I said, getting impatient, but keeping it friendly in case it turned out to be Sylvia, or a member of the Cambridgeshire constabulary. Whoever it was shouldn't have been walking round rivers at midnight and I felt like telling them so; decent folk were in their beds. Except me, of course, but I had my reasons.

But it wasn't Sylvia, or the Cambridgeshire constabulary. I know, because it changed the torch over in its hands, fumbled with something for a moment, and there followed a bang.

A bullet-type bang.

I didn't spend time waiting for him to have another shot. I took to the heather, or rather, there being no heather to take to, I set off swiftly in the direction of Miss Clew's car, underpants and all.

The hunt was up, but the hunter had the advantage, because he had acquired a bicycle from somewhere, and came after me on it.

Into the bushes where a bicycle can't go, I thought. Cunning weaving, I thought. So I weaved cunningly into the bushes and found myself up to the waist in very smelly water with a great big bramble wound round my throat.

The worst was yet to come. Suck air through a reed, the textbook says, but I didn't have a reed, so I took a deep breath and stuck my head under anyway, hoping for the best. I was coming up for the second time when I caught a glimpse of my assailant through the undergrowth, a glimpse I could have done without.

Searching for me with torch and gun, intent on the hunt, bald head a-glitter in the moonlight, was Joe Keough.

Dead Joe Keough, shot down in a Dublin backyard, before my very eyes.

I stayed in the water for a long time, feeling most upset. It was not pleasant and it was very cold, but this latest apparition was too much for me. I stayed where I was for at least an hour, risking pleurisy and double pneumonia and all sorts of things until I was quite certain dead Joe had gone away.

Unfortunately he had gone away with my clothes in his bicycle basket, for which I didn't thank him. I thought I should cut back to the car where Sylvia Clews would be waiting shamefaced, having failed me in my hour of need; but when I got there there was no Sylvia to be seen, and likewise no car.

Breaking with tradition to rendezvous with Alice Alexander in Cambridge was one thing, getting ditched by her minion and chased along a river bank by someone I'd seen shot was quite another, I decided, as I padded through the dark streets of Cambridge looking for the Salvation Army, where at least they would provide a rope to sleep on, though rope sleeping is not a system I can recommend. M.2 and Alice had a lot to answer for, putting the whole combined operation at risk, not to speak of false Sylvia who would at that very moment, I trusted, be getting a tongue lashing from Alice for losing me. In the morning I was going straight round to Magdalene to complain, before setting forth for my London rendezvous with evil William Talbot.

'Now then,' said the tall blue voice in my ear.

'Good morning officer,' I said, pretending I was an athlete and skipping gamely up and down.

'Having trouble?' he asked politely, leaning his bicycle against the wall and groping for his notebook.

I wondered faintly if he could have me for running without lights ... in a flash reflecting that I'd nowhere to hang one.

'Can't run round the streets like that y'know,' he said, gravely. 'Not in your Y-fronts, no sir.'

'It was,' I said, in a flash of pure inspiration, 'a jape, a student jape.'

'Bit long in the tooth for that, aren't you sir?'

I drew myself up, with some dignity, I may say. Considering my cold state I think I acted positively courageously. But they were Carnaby Street briefs, not Y-fronts, and I wanted him to see that I was hand in glove with the swinging aristocracy, none of your red brick riff-raff up for the day.

'Take me to the station,' I said, talking a bold line. 'This is a matter of national security.'

I could see I'd taken the wind out of his sails. He looked worried, and fiddled with his pencil.

'There'll be a charge of course,' he said, undaunted.

'Oh,' I said. It was an aspect which hadn't occurred to me, because in Earls Court I'd have got off with a caution, being known to the police as a partygoer-of-renown ever since Dymphna's twenty-first in the lift. Compared to Dymphna's twenty-first this was child's play. I stopped skipping up and down because it obviously carried no weight with him. The Market Square at two in the morning was remarkably uninviting as the moon shone on W. H. Smith and my hairy chest indiscriminately.

A monk, or at least someone dressed as a monk, slipped quietly by in the shadows.

'They are not,' I said, pointing at him, 'allowed to dress up like that because of Henry VIII. Why don't you arrest him?' I was trying to imply that his was the more heinous offence, but it didn't go down well. The policeman offered me his cape, in the interests of modesty.

'Now sir,' he said. 'What have you been taking?'

I think he took me for the limp end of an orgy.

The policeman and I plodded through darkened Cambridge, which I found very picturesque. I'd never been there before and would undoubtedly have appreciated it more if I hadn't been hobbling along in my bare feet, leaving a damp trail on the pavement behind me, but the town came out of it remarkably well for all that. Place to visit when I'm rich, I thought, and filed it accordingly.

'Cold night,' the policeman said in a fatherly voice, just to show there was no animosity.

'Very,' I said, thinking what a splendid place it was, just the spot to cradle our future King, although there was no sign of him, or any other flowers of British youth for that matter; they must all have been tucked up in their little beds or burning the midnight electricity. What I did see was a shabby crowd of beatniks sprawled in the doorway of a chemist's shop, one of the nice ones with the big coloured bottles they won't sell you however much you pay. What a let down for Britain, I thought. What if I had

been a Wog tourist, or a French television camera-
man trying to prove Britain would shop the Common
Market? It only needed a subtle sub-title and Charles
would be in there grovelling with them.

'You should do something about them,' I said to my
policeman, very much on my British dignity, clasping
his cape tightly round me to stop the shivers.

To his everlasting credit he took my point, un-
latched his notebook pocket and started across the
road to them. I tiptoed gingerly in the rear, because
the roadway was even colder on the feet than the
pavement.

'Now then,' he said, which was obviously his standard script whatever the action, 'Having trouble?'

There were four of them, but they proved to be a
bit long in the tooth for beatniks so I took them for
displaced intellectuals revisiting the scene of past
triumphs, when there had been a boat race. They rose
as one and stood there in their rags, looking at us in
awe.

'Move along now, if you please,' the policeman
said, being very lenient I thought, considering the
way he'd talked to me.

Three of them came forward mouthing horribly.
One twisted the arm of the law behind its back, one
hit him the stomach, and the third applied a little
white pad to the policeman's face.

Then they all looked at me menacingly.

CHAPTER NINE

I did my best to look like a beautiful person, or at the very worst a firm believer in non-violence. I'd had quite enough for one night, as far as I was concerned somebody else could have a go.

'Take him away,' someone said, from the shadows of the shop doorway.

The three violent rag bags hoisted the policeman between them and walked away into the gloom, leaving me with the ruthless ringleader.

'How are you, lamb?' Grace asked.

'Very cold,' I said, retaining my composure very well, all things considered.

She said that in that case we'd better go inside before I caught a chill, and opened the shop door to admit me.

We filed past glass cabinets and the lovely bottles into a back room just off the dispensary. I sat on the sofa and shivered whilst Grace lit the gas fire. She very kindly gave me the blanket she'd been wrapped up in to put around me.

'Too bad about Miss Clews,' she said, by way of light conversation that was meant to smite me where it hurt.

'As far as I am concerned,' I said, with cold dignity, 'Miss Sylvia Clews is out, but out.' Lush lady or not, I said, she had a duty to M.2 and dumping me on the river bank to be shot at just because she had last minute virginal qualms wasn't part of it.

'She was only doing her job,' Grace said, no longer able to restrain the rabbit teeth, which appeared nipping her lip. She said I wasn't to think it was anything personal. 'You must try not to get all worked up about it. I'm sure she thought you were quite nice really, in other circumstances she might have gone through with it.'

'What do you mean, "other circumstances",' I snapped, drawing the blanket around me.

'If she hadn't been working for Eternity,' Grace said.

'Oh,' I said.

Grace was obviously enjoying herself very much, as she usually does when she's telling me what really happened. If only she would tell me before it happens I could join the party, but she never does. She sat there giving me the flashing eyes and the teeth and saying I was getting to be quite a Rudolph wasn't I?

I said I thought I was catching cold.

'In that case,' she said, 'you'd better go upstairs and put some clothes on.'

This seemed a good idea, so upstairs I went. She'd been very thoughtful and had laid out a suit on the bed, with shirts and socks and all the paraphernalia. The colouring was very conservative and not what I'm accustomed to, being something of a trendsetter in my modest way, but it was nice to get the suede boots on, the fleecy lining worked wonders for my poor feet. I dressed myself and inspected the Baxter miniatures, which are worth having if you like little pictures of Balmoral and the Royals of yesteryear, but only fetch a pittance on the market, though they may come back. With the suit on and my hair back at its best I admired myself in the mirror. Being blown up, recuperating in Wog-land and eating tapioca and runner beans in Bracknell might have weakened a lesser man, but I was right back on the top of my form, even though the scar on my arm sometimes itched.

'Very nice,' Grace said from the door. 'Becomes you much better than all that hippy gear. Now you look your age.'

I ignored the slighting reference to my excellent dress sense and said that it was very thoughtful of her to look it out for me, even if it was a little outmoded. I said these little things showed the people who really care as apart from the gold diggers like Sylvia Clews, whom I'd been trying to pump about Eternity, which was why I'd chatted her up. I thought it sounded quite convincing, but Grace didn't seem to think so.

'To keep you straight,' Grace said, 'Miss Clews isn't Miss Clews at all.'

I said that that was quite all right. I was too old a hand to expect anybody who had anything to do with the business to use their own name, it isn't the done thing. I said I even had an alias of my own, of which I was very proud.

'She's Mrs. Percy Smith,' Grace said. I said that that was very nice for little Percy, whom I wouldn't honestly have thought to be in the same league as sensuous Sylvia, from what I'd seen of him in the bar of the Daid. He was, I informed her, a dab hand at driving little train engines, but apart from that a colourless conformist.

'Sylvia used to work for the French,' Grace said. 'That is before she sold out to Eternity. There are some who say that she married Percy as a matter of convenience, Percy being in with the management.'

I straightened my borrowed tie and thought about it. Despite my experience on the Cam I found it difficult to think evil of nice Sylvia, at least personal evil as opposed to the routine cloak and dagger kind that made up day to day living.

'Actually,' I said, 'I had quite a battle down there. I had to take on two of them, barehanded.'

'Sylvia was unaccompanied,' Grace said.

'Joe Keough was there,' I said.

She laughed and said she understood I'd been going round telling Vikdor's people that Joe Keough was dead, so how could Joe Keough be there?

'He was,' I said, firmly.

She said I was making too much of a good thing out of it. I could have him dead or not dead, but not both ways.

'Those Keoughs are very tricky,' I said. 'They're like you, they keep turning up. I don't trust them and I don't think Vikdor does either.'

'Oh?' Grace said.

'Vikdor doesn't even believe there *is* a Joe Keough,' I said. 'So there you are. He says Maggie hasn't got a brother.'

'If you were Vikdor,' Grace said, 'and it crossed your mind that your Dublin agent might have sold out to the opposition, what would you do?'

'Send somebody independent in to check,' I said.

'And if you were the Dublin agent, or the brother of the Dublin agent, what would you do about the somebody?'

'Take him down by the Cam and shoot him,' I said, getting it in one.

'I think you'd better tell me exactly what you are supposed to be doing about Eternity, and why Vikdor pulls the strings while M.2 do the work,' Grace said.

'I don't think I'm allowed to tell you that,' I said. Then, somewhat self-consciously, but not without malicious glee, I quoted the Official Secrets Act at her.

'As far as I can see,' Grace said, 'M.2 have made another one of their botched deals.'

'It is a joint enterprise,' I said, stiffly.

'Is it?' she said.

'One operative from both sides,' I said.

'You and Lefle,' she said.

'Yes.'

'*Both* from M.2,' she said.

I allowed myself a guileless smile. What she didn't realise, I explained, was that although we were both from M.2 Leather Vikdor didn't know that. Leather Vikdor thought that I was Garvey, and that I was working for him. M.2, I told her, were tying Vikdor up in little knots.

She said that if she was trying to pass herself off as an exiled Russian she wouldn't go complaining to people about Wog food when they served up Russian national dishes.

I felt a sudden chill. 'Bearded Nana?' I said.

'Bearded Nana,' she said.

I tried to think back over the weeks I'd spent in

Bearded Nana's care before I realised she wasn't an Irish nun. All sorts of things came back, remarks about being a Briton with the National Health behind me and Thomas Hardy in Wog bindings. It didn't sound like dialogue typical of the cousin of a Russian count, I had to admit it.

'How do you get to know all these things?' I said.

She said she had her sources.

I sat down on the bed, feeling somewhat depressed.

'I think we may assume that Vikdor knows who you are,' Grace said, 'which means that M.2 have made their customary mess of things. Vikdor doesn't have to risk anything, beyond a little foreign exchange. In return M.2 investigates Eternity for him, in the process checking the integrity of his own agent, Maggie Keough, while Vikdor sits back and twiddles his thumbs. Investigating your own agents is always a touchy business, they are liable to turn on you. I'm sure he'll be delighted to have it done for him.'

I said Alice wasn't going to like it.

'Don't you dare tell Alice,' Grace said.

'Why not?' I said.

'Because I want to,' Grace said.

The sun burned high in the morning sky as we left the Cambridge chemist's to keep my appointment with Mr. William Talbot of Shepherd's Bush, the mercenary who was to be instrumental in the combined operation which Vikdor had viciously twisted to his own benefit. The sky was blue and there wasn't a sign of the snow of yesterday or the nasty nip that had been in the air the night before. It was a perfect day for writing my name large in the annals of organised large-scale British crime, which was what I was about to do.

'I hope you have a car,' I said, thinking that it would be a bit of a rush if we had to take the train. My appointment with William Talbot was fixed for Bermondsey Market in the early hours and I couldn't afford to be late.

'Don't worry about it,' Grace said, 'I'm sure that we'll pick one up somewhere.'

I didn't like the sound of that. I was quite cross with her. I said that there was no point in being vicious for the sake of it, and practically accused her of getting a kick out of it. Why couldn't she buy her own car on the H.P. like everybody else, instead of persistently pinching other people's?

'Get in,' she said, opening a car door.

So I got in.

'All right?' she said, trying her collection of keys in the ignition.

'I have no choice, have I?' I said.

'No,' she said.

I could quite see why M.2 looked down on her, behaving like that. British Agents are honest, in their fashion.

'Personal possessions don't mean a thing to you, do they?' I said bitterly.

She said if I squirmed round any more I would damage the little Baxter prints in my pocket, and then I wouldn't be able to get a good price for them, would I?

'I must have picked them up by accident,' I said.

She smiled unpleasantly in the driving mirror as we cruised up Trumpington Street.

'Turn the car round,' I said. 'These prints got into my pocket quite inadvertently. I was looking at them when you called and must have rushed down stairs without thinking. I must put them back where they belong. I certainly had no intention of purloining them, and to suggest I had is a reflection on you, Grace dear, not on me. I have my standards, strange as it may seem.'

She said that we couldn't go back because of the man in the shop.

'Why not?' I said.

Because he might be upset at seeing us again, she said.

'I thought he was a friend of yours,' I said, in a voice which must have echoed my misgivings.

She said she was sure he wouldn't really mind what had happened, whoever he was. So much for being thoughtful and providing nice clothes for me, and a place to lay my head. At any moment a nude chemist might have marched upstairs with the police and arrested us both.

I pointed this out.

She said that that wasn't possible, because he'd been unconscious under the counter all night, so what was I getting all het up about?

'Little pink pills?' I said.

'His own,' she said, and the symmetry of it seemed to please her.

'This,' I said, in my conspiratorial voice, 'is Gerald Arthur Otley. I wish to speak with Miss Alexander on a matter of urgency please.'

I sensed a new note of respect in the day girl's click as she put me through.

'Alice,' I barked, 'is it safe to talk?'

'You are not supposed to ring me up,' she said. 'You are supposed to be working for Vikdor. If you go on like this you'll blow your cover.'

'But is Vikdor to be trusted?' I snapped.

'Yes,' she said.

'I don't think so,' I said.

'You mean that Grace doesn't think so,' she said.

There was a lengthy pause whilst I digested this. In the transport café behind me Grace sat eating sausage, egg and chips, all unconcerned. She thought I was ringing up Heindleighter to make arrangements about the Irish knick-knacks for Chloe which I hadn't got. It hurt me to deceive her, but Britain came first and also Bandy Alice might pay me for it. This was the theory, but it didn't seem to be turning out quite as planned.

'Why should Vikdor suspect anything?' Alice said, impatiently. 'You haven't slipped up, have you?'

'No, indeed no,' I said. Well I couldn't tell her about taking Nana for a nun, could I? It was a perfectly understandable mistake, but not the sort of thing with which she would sympathise.

'In any case,' Alice said, 'you should be getting on with things. With or without Vikdor, we can't stop now. We've got to know if they've got Bloody Mary.'

'Yes,' I said.

'And you can tell Grace,' Alice said, '*if*, by any chance, she is at your elbow, which I strongly suspect,

that M.2 is quite capable of handling this without her
assistance. I may as well point out to you that we dis-
approve of her very strongly. It would be in your
interest not to associate with that young woman if you
can help it, these things do not go unnoticed.'

'You've got it all wrong,' I said. 'Grace is pro-us. It
is Vikdor you ought to worry about.'

'You leave Vikdor to me,' Alice said, and the line
went dead. I could just see her sitting in her moth-
eaten cardigan clicking her false teeth and polishing
the coffee cup. In contrast nifty Grace was much more
to my liking, quite apart from being sexy.

I left the kiosk and came across to the table. Grace
had finished eating and was doing up her eyes.

'Get through?' she asked.

'Yes.'

'Alice say anything?'

'What?'

'Did you have to pay anything?'

I gave her a frown of deep suspicion and sat down
beside my cold toast and dejected mushrooms. I was
pretty certain in my own mind that she had asked
about Alice, but I couldn't be sure. She was giving me
the tooth treatment again as she clipped the little
brush on to the back of the mirror and folded the
whole thing into the back of her lipstick. It was most
ingenious.

'Where did you get that?' I said.

'A man,' she said.

I looked hurt, but tried to be brave about it.

'How do I look?' she asked.

'Ravishing,' I said, vindictively resolving not to tell
her about the smudge on her cheek.

'Thank you,' she said.

We cruised by the Elephant and Castle, very much
not my spiritual home, all tiled tunnels and office
blocks with the nice pearly kings and queens
wiped off the map, not that I'm gone on pearly kings
and queens, but I do stick up for the Heritage. If you
get lost in their little tunnels now you stay lost, because all the tiles look the same.

'Infanta of Castile,' I said, dropping a tit bit of
London lore which I was sure would impress her,
though I sometimes wonder about Grace and the
finer things.

'You have not told me what you are supposed to be
doing in your joint operation yet,' Grace said. 'I think
it would be a good idea if you did, just in case I have
to come and get you out of it.'

'Sorry,' I said, 'orders.'

Actually I rather enjoyed saying it, because Grace
is always taking unfair advantage of me by concealing
vital information. It was a pleasant change to have the
positions reversed.

'William Talbot,' she said, musing. 'Now what do I
know about William Talbot?'

'Nasty big man,' I said. 'Neolithic club-swinger,
drags ladies home by the hair. Not your sort dear.'

'I don't know,' she said, 'I like a man who is a
man.'

I said that there was a case to be made for intellect
and the aesthetic life and she wouldn't really fancy
William Talbot if she had him around the house on
Sundays. I said he was nasty, bribery and corruption
and everything.

'How much did you get?' she asked.

I said that I was incorruptible.

She smiled sweetly.

'Well I didn't tell him the truth anyway,' I said. 'He wanted to know who was paying and I told him Eternity and I said they were the I.R.A. I think it was very quick of me.' I didn't say she would be proud of me, because I thought that went without saying.

'I suppose it never occurred to you that he might check up?' she asked me.

I said that I didn't see how he could do that. I said she was being unnecessarily alarmist, I had everything under control.

She shrugged her shoulders and stopped the car. 'I'd better leave you off, lamb,' she said. 'Just in case they've got the number down at the police station. It would never do to have you picked up for joy-riding in your finest hour.'

I looked at the dismal pavement with evident displeasure, which I did not attempt to conceal. It wasn't my London at all, no swinging boutiques, hippy hats, nobody who faintly resembled a Beatle or Jane Asher, just dingy brick walls and blue and pink modern flats with the look of doom upon them ... future generations are going to love our architects.

'Where is Bermondsey?' I demanded sternly, retaining my seat in the face of her teeth.

'I thought you would know,' she said, 'being such an enthusiastic Londoner.'

I said I got on the bus with my bag and sat there till the market appeared. I didn't go slumming west of the river, I was a flower person.

'Remind me to talk to you about that sometime,' she said,

I told her I was positively the King of the Chelsea Antique Market, the indoor one. After they'd had their little teas on the balcony upstairs all the gay young things came down to see me, because I'd had my picture in the *Evening Standard*. She didn't ask me why I'd had my picture in the *Evening Standard* so I had to tell her. It isn't everyone, I said proudly, it isn't everyone who has sold a piece of genuine Spanish lace to Mick Jagger.

I could see that she was envious, but I didn't press it.

'I've been thinking about your collaborator, William Talbot,' she said, 'I've just remembered what it is that he does for a living.'

'Oh yes,' I said, innocently.

'He organises jailbreaks,' she said. 'Doesn't he?'

CHAPTER TEN

I strode confidently into the market, looking for William Talbot, jailbreaker extraordinary, and also for someone to whom I could sell the Baxter prints. Stalls stretched in serried ranks before me, filled with lovely foolish things that I wanted for my own, and antiquarian tat. Then I saw my friend Charles who had an exquisite piece of soapstone, which might just serve to pacify Chloe.

Clutching my prints I pushed forward to his stall. Ask for thirty shillings each, I told myself, expect fifteen.

'Hallo Charles,' I cried casually, as if nothing was further from my mind than the cut and thrust of our habitual haggles.

'Go away,' Charles said, in an urgent whisper. 'What do you want to show your face here for?'

After all I'd done for Charles I thought he was laying it on a bit thick. Admittedly we had had a little dispute over the dragon I lost in the Victoria and Albert, but that could have happened to anybody and it wasn't Ming or anything like it, whatever Aussie Harry said. I was about to tell him what I thought of him in the blunt honest manner which marks me, when I saw a distant blob in a brown fur coat which was unmistakably Heindleighter, to whom I owed a lot of money.

'Thank you Charles,' I said warmly, and strolled away past the tin-box man and the sex change from Droitwich. Good old Charles, a pal indeed. I couldn't afford to meet Heindleighter in case he got over-excited and vicious, in which case word would fly to Chloe, who might cut me off without a further penny if it did. Being cut off without a penny would mean selling my Festival of Britain souvenirs, which I regard as an investment for my old age.

I hid behind a stall full of old medical journals, spectacles and riding boots which shouldn't have been there at all by normal Bermondsey standards, being a market for the élite. Two ladies in cloaks and brown trousers were discussing their dog and a sale in Gloucester, while a cadaverous man complained to a lovely little lady. 'I can't stand his bowing,' he said. 'I told them to put me next to Ricky.'

I smiled at them both. She smiled straight back at me, obviously an innocent, but her pale friend didn't deign to notice.

'Tell that to Wally,' the girl said. She had the sort of knees I feel at home with. 'Wally's bowing is atrocious.'

Then William Talbot strode past, carrying a gilt mirror as if it was a matchbox. I followed obediently in his wake, towards the large grey van he had commandeered for the job.

William got into the back with the mirror, and I clambered in after him. 'You're late,' he said, rounding on me.

I was busy inspecting his Rockingham cottage and wondering who had made it for him. It was wrong, and I felt rather pleased about it because of the way

113

he'd rubbed in my Portuguese box. I wasn't altogether sure what was wrong, but I knew it wasn't
right, being pretty good on Rockingham cottages. I
hoped he thought it was a good piece, so that I could
dazzle him.

'Your Rockingham cottage isn't,' I said, boldly
taking the offensive.

'Get into the front, and be quick about it,' he said,
taking the cottage from me and putting it into his
market bag. He was obviously shaken, and didn't want
me asking awkward questions. It was the sort of thing
he could never foist on the discerning British public,
it would go straight off to the States via his shippers. I
had a friend called Irwin Shaw who shipped to an
American called Driffield and we made a lot of un-
taxable income until Irwin forgot to pay for the
Adam fireplace. He didn't exactly forget to pay for
the Adam fireplace; he rented a flat with an Adam
fireplace in it and when he moved out the fireplace
moved with him. The upshot was that Irwin had to
live in Galway where no one knew him and I lost
touch with Driffield, a grievous blow.

We got into the front, William looking very grim
as he settled by the wheel.

'If you're trying to foul up this operation,' he said,
carefully tugging on his rubber gloves, 'you are going
the right way about it. As a result of waiting here for
you we are far behind schedule. We can't afford to be.
So shut up and sit still.'

A little explanation seemed called for. I would
have been all right if Grace had left me somewhere
civilised, as I started to tell him, but he didn't
seem to be interested. So I thought I'd tell him

114

about my adventure on the Cam, just to pass the time.

'Somebody tried to shoot me last night,' I said, impressively. 'Or rather, very early this morning.'

'Where?'

'On the Cam.'

'Who?'

'Three large men and a lady called Sylvia,' I said, thinking how much better it sounded with three large men instead of one. The shock of it being dead Joe Keough about equalled three as far as panic went, so I felt justified in my little lie, which was only to make the story more entertaining.

'Did you get them?' he said, adjusting the driving mirror casually, as if everybody clobbered three large men who tried to shoot them.

I said that I was in no condition to get anybody. I was in my underpants and dripping wet.

'Why?' he asked, with Shepherds Bush bonhomie.

'There are things that a gentleman does not discuss,' I said, with dignity.

'Why?' he demanded, menacing me with a porcelain shepherdess he held in his free hand, whilst steering deftly with the other. At least I thought he was menacing me, but in fact he was groping for the Phensic he kept in her basket, as good a place to keep it as any I suppose.

'I felt like a swim,' I said.

'As you will,' he said, recognising in me a master of tact, not to be outflanked by a small-time operator.

'What do I have to do today?' I said, with a delicious thrill of anticipation at being a bad man without having to feel guilty about it.

'You'll do exactly what you are told,' he said.

It was the sort of cottage where I could have set up as T. E. Lawrence, if I'd felt inclined that way. Around it stretched the barren moorland, nature in the raw, diluted only by the three cars William's men had pinched for the operation. We finished spraying them and went inside to watch William Talbot's film show which was full of blow-up shots of the prison walls and maps of the moor and the timetables they were all to adhere to. In between there were filthy films, just to keep us awake.

'Very good William,' I said. 'You got that from the Ipcress File didn't you?'

'What?' William said.

I turned away in despair.

We sat on upturned boxes and played dour games of cards. We synchronised our watches and talked about filthy Dolores, who had done one of us down. We ate baked beans from tins heated up on William Talbot's primus. I for one felt mean and rugged, tie askew, out-to-get-the-cop-who-crossed-me.

In threes William's men left the cottage and drove off to their appointed destinations, mud plastered all over their number plates. At last I was alone with the leader.

'Congratulations William,' I said. 'I like your nasty friends.'

But William was busy packing the tear-gas cylinders in the back seat, and didn't hear me.

'Wake up,' he said, prodding his elbow into my stitches. I'd been having a lovely dream about finding a lot of opaline that someone was giving away; a dream which can't have been unrelated to nearly bumping into Heindleighter, which always has something of a traumatic effect, though not usually such a pleasant one.

It was very cold in the van, despite being an evening in spring. I've always had a soft spot for so-called frisky lambs, hopping round to keep warm, but I couldn't help but envy William his thick woollen sweater.

We were parked with the lights off, the moor pitch dark all around us, the moon luckily having an off night. Soon we were going in to bust things up and make a diversion while car three dashed in to pick up the extra passenger who had no right to be going anywhere.

'What's wrong?' I said.

'I want you to go across to Alan,' he said. 'There's been a change of plan.'

'Oh great,' I said. 'Stumble about the moor in the darkness, risking life and limb in bog holes. Why not use the radio?'

He said that we were observing radio silence. He said somebody had to tell Alan to take car two to the West Gate, and we couldn't risk another transmission in case somebody picked it up.

'You go,' I said.

He said he was the C.O., he couldn't go. I was just an onlooker, I was expendable.

'I'm paying,' I said, snappily.

'Your friends are paying,' he said. 'They won't be pleased if we muck it up, will they?'

Alice would kill me, because jailbreaking is one of

117

the things M.2 doesn't do, so when we did do it we had to get it right, because it would never do to let the common constabulary get one up on us by foiling the attempt. It had to work, or Alice's wrath would be awful to behold.

'I'll go,' I said, accepting the lesser of two evils.

'Are you sure you can manage?' he said.

I resented the slur on my trekking ability and told him so. Head of Yellow Six, I'd been, back in my cubbing days, when I could tell an oak from an elm without looking at the name under the picture, and also knot things.

'Good,' he said, and gave me very detailed instructions for Alan, which I absorbed faithfully, feeling brave. Then I climbed out of the car and stood shivering as the wind stroked the heather.

'I don't think I know which way is North,' I said, peering around me. 'Can't I take a torch or something?'

He said no, for obvious reasons. Then he shook my hand and wished me good luck, obviously thinking I was a gallant fellow.

'I can cope, boss,' I said, gamely, and faced off into the freezing night.

There was no suggestion of a path, not even a goat one. Neither was there a moon to help me on my way. I harboured all sorts of fears about breaking my ankles, which have never been very strong, and lying dying on the moor whilst savage sheep ate me. Savage sheep were a new concept, and the more I thought about them the less I liked what I was doing.

It was then, and only then, that I began to wonder about the change of plan. *Why* had there been a

118

change of plan? We were on radio silence, there could be no new information. Puzzled, I trotted on, sure that William knew what he was doing, being the original getaway person.

I had made about three hundred yards when William switched on the engine of our mobile H.Q. 'Hey,' I shouted, abandoning our compulsory caution. 'Where do you think you are going?'

I started running back towards him. This turned out to be a bad idea, because my foot caught on a rock and I went over on my face. By the time I got up our H.Q. was just a rumble in the distance, driven without lights.

A cold wind stung the heather scratches on my face and my stitches began to throb, even though they'd all been taken out weeks before.

William had double-crossed me. I hoped it meant fun for William, but it didn't make much sense to me. The plan would go ahead as in the original outline, with the extra passenger shipped off to Dublin with the right sort of reputation behind him, and later on I would report William to the proper authority. It seemed a great deal of trouble to go to just to leave me stranded in the middle of nowhere, where the sheep could harry me.

I gave up trying to work it out. Eternity might have got at him, but why should they? Eternity didn't even know he existed. The dangerous bit of our operation was supposed to be when we got our extra passenger to Dublin, hand picked for feeding into their operation. It was only to give him the sort of pedigree they would appreciate that we'd switched Lefle for an atom spy in the first place, and the only people who knew about that were the top brass at M.2, Alice, Lefle, Vikdor and me. There could have been no leakage.

I was pondering this when something exploded. Car one had gone into action. The sound came reverberating across the moor, followed almost instantaneously by the first howl of the sirens. It all added up to an unpleasant shock, because I was supposed to be miles away from the scene of the action, and obviously I wasn't.

Flashing lights everywhere, a cordon of uniformed gentlemen tramping across the moor, mobile floodlights on vans, dogs barking. It was only three-quarters of an hour since the first siren, but already the hunt was up with a vengeance. I hadn't helped myself by running desperately to escape from the danger area, but running in circles. Once I'd arrived at the top of a hill and seen some of the prison buildings below me, with the great big hole in the wall that we'd planned for, so I had reason to believe that William's operation had gone off successfully, but I anticipated some little difficulty in explaining to the nice warders that I'd had nothing to do with it.

William had dumped me with evil cunning. His idea was obviously to use me as a further diversion. Presumably he had checked my story about the I.R.A. and decided to get his own back, so Grace had been right again. I had no illusions about my fate. M.2 would be sad to see me put away for helping jail-breakers, but their man at Holyhead would hand over the money when Lefle was delivered, with or without me. William would have a plausible reason for leaving me to my fate and nobody would want to know me, understandably enough.

There didn't seem to be much I could do about this state of affairs, bar running for my life before the police cordon arrived. I'd already tried that and found it didn't work, owing to my faulty sense of direction. Now the cordon had come there was at least something to run away from, but the chance had gone. I was back almost where I'd started, crouching behind a rock and wheezing. Further running was beyond me in the frail condition induced by my recent experiences and was doomed to almost certain failure anyway. The night air carried all too clearly the sounds of the hunt, dogs whined and men shouted. Already policemen would be throwing up road blocks and farmers locking up their daughters.

What to do? I could walk in and surrender, but that struck me as defeatist. The only reasonable alternative was to hide somewhere where the dogs might miss me, so I thought I might try that.

All the best escapers hide in haystacks and are discovered by astonished ploughboys with dirty great forks, but there wasn't a haystack in sight, not even a little one. Come to think of it I've never seen a haystack on a moor, so I think they must be planted by accomplices when likely to be called for.

Time to move again, because they were coming down the hill towards my rock.

I scuttled away, looking for another to hide behind. But this time I didn't scuttle very far, because I put my foot out and stepped on nothing, which immediately settled my problem.

I found myself upside down in a stony culvert, which might once have had a stream to call its own but hadn't any more. It seemed a shrewd move to stay put so I set to arranging the heather overhead into rudimentary cover and, with that done, lay down on my back and started piling small rocks on top of myself.

It was an idea worthy of me, a tribute to my agile brain, which, even under stress, could come up with a potential winner. In the darkness I was going to pass for a mound of rocks left unattended, the nearest I could get to a haystack with the material to hand.

Self-interred, I lay there waiting for the worst, not altogether without hope.

The worst was a long time coming, so that I grew quite impatient, wanting it over with if I was going to get clobbered, anything to end the suspense. Things weren't helped by a certain dampness that pervaded, coupled with inconsiderate rocks which prodded me in places where they had no license to prod.

I'll never know the exact sequence of events overhead, but the effect down below was disastrous. I suppose one of them followed my example and stepped out into the air, he really should have been more careful where he was going. I heard a shout, and something inhumanly heavy crunched on top of the stones that I'd arranged so carefully over my stomach.

It was too much, much too much.

I sat up abruptly, sending my stones rattling in all directions.

Then I should have done something brilliant like hitting the large man and making a break for it, and I would have, if I'd been able to breathe. As it was I sat there and wheezed at him politely.

But he didn't wheeze back at me, for he was out cold.

'Something's happened to that bloke,' somebody said, overhead.

So I grabbed the unconscious man's little cap and stuck it on my head and stood up, warily.

'You all right?' a friendly voice asked, flashing his torch at me.

'Had a bit of a fall,' I said, and clambered out of the ditch. Willing arms helped me, and luckily nobody noticed the dark shadow in the pit below, which at any moment might be up and after me.

'I think you'd better go back,' one of them said. 'You look a bit shaken.'

I said something heroic and straightened the large man's cap, so that it hid as much of my face as possible.

'I don't think I know you,' one of them said. 'Who're you with?'

'Central,' I said recklessly.

'In that case,' one of them said, 'what are you doing over here?'

'Lost,' I said, which was true enough.

'Come along there, sharpen up,' somebody shouted from the right, a voice of authority. 'No hanging about.'

'Don't bother to wait for me,' I said, 'you go on, I'll just stay here and rest.'

They seemed a bit doubtful about it, but on they went, and back into the ditch I went, having a conscience about leaving the poor man to the elements.

He was still unconscious, but breathing and on the way to recovery. So I got him up out of the ditch and left him propped up against a rock where they were bound to find him. Then I borrowed his official coat to add to the cap and tied his hands and feet together with his braces.

'Sorry,' I said, as he stirred a little, but it was no time for regrets, and I set off at a quick trot over the moor towards the nearest set of car lights, which turned out to be a landrover.

'I'm from Central,' I said to the brawny policeman at the wheel. 'What are you doing here?'

'I was told to . . .'

'Nonsense,' I barked. 'You people never learn do you? Show me your credentials immediately.'

So he showed me his little white card and I looked at it. 'I'll keep this for the moment,' I said, with all the authority I could muster. 'You're wanted at Central at once.'

'Where?' he said, which was a very reasonable question.

'Over there,' I said, wildly pointing in the direction where there seemed to be fewest torches flashing about, and therefore least chance of contradiction. 'Go at once. I'll take care of the car.'

He looked a bit dubious, but he went all the same, and was well out of the way by the time I clambered in and started her up, on my way to freedom.

CHAPTER ELEVEN

I sat in Amanda's café, glumly surveying my sausage roll and chips and doing my best to hide behind my *Daily Mail*.

GETAWAY PEOPLE STRIKE AGAIN it said, in stark black letters. H-BOMB TRAITOR IN DRAMATIC JAILBREAK. A large photograph of top nuclear physicist Edmund Black at his trial was inset below, to which some obliging expert had made a few adjustments. Now Lefle would pass for him adequately, granted the effects of eight years behind bars. The picture of the hole in the wall of the jail was very nice too, obviously our stuff had gone off to order. Not a word about me. I might as well not have been in on it, instead of being the mastermind. If they'd realised I'd gone off with one of their landrovers they were being very quiet about it, which I suppose was not unreasonable.

I felt quite indignant.

I looked over my paper at the large tin fence across the way, and the wooden gates which bore the legend 'Wm. Talbot, West Ken. Yard', which accounted for my presence. I was going to give Wm. Talbot a bit of my mind.

'You want something more?' the lady said.

Gracefully, I declined her offer. She took away my

125

cup, still half full of her tepid tea. Then she stood by the counter shuffling her feet.

I smiled and turned over to the Dog selections.

'Fred,' she called.

That sort of person is always enormous, and Fred was no exception.

'Been here an hour and a quarter Fred,' she said. 'Sausage roll and chips, cup of tea. Looking at me ... you know.'

Fred nodded happily.

'Madam,' I said, rising as Fred ambled forward.

'Better chuck it son,' he said, holding the door open for me. I was going to tell him his wife was over-sexed, but I thought better of it, and anyway at that moment William's large grey van came round the corner. I stood reading the advertisements for Strict Correction by Stern Ladies in the window of the vegetarian shop next door as the van turned in through the gates, which were firmly closed behind it.

Walking in on William seemed ill advised, in case he still had some of his jailbreakers with him, who might just possibly be persuaded to wrap me up in a carpet and float me down the Thames. So I decided on the indirect approach, heading for the gate of the scrapyard next door. I walked confidently through the gates prepared to ask for a hip bath if anybody stopped me. It could do no harm, you can always find a market for a hip bath. As it was, I went untackled, and found my way to the wall over a mountain of old cars and gas cookers. I settled myself behind what was left of an Austin, just in time to witness a further example of the nastiness of which my friend William was capable.

126

The large grey van was parked in the yard. William stood beside it, supervising the loading. There was nothing reprehensible about this in principle, it was what they were loading that appalled the Briton in me ... a tall well-dressed corpse. At least I took it for a corpse from the way William's aides were loading it. They dropped it hard on the back of the van and it didn't stir a muscle, poor thing. One more corpse might not have made much difference one way or the other, you get used to having them around, but this corpse was special. Even at that distance I could see that it bore more than a passing resemblance to Vikdor.

Vikdor was on my side, technically ... at least I think he was supposed to be, but I was getting a little confused. *I* was on Vikdor's side, so long as we were investigating Eternity. It was if and when we got round to investigating Bloody Mary that I ceased to be on his side. Then I was on M.2's, if I wasn't on Grace's. But everybody was supposed to be paying me, so it was probably all right.

William climbed into the front of the van and I started clambering down the Austin to the ground, with brave ideas about intercepting him. I had to be sure that Vikdor was dead before I went ringing up Alice to tell her so, because if there was any mistake Alice wasn't going to love me any more.

'You can't do that,' the man shouted, from his little hut.

I sped for the gates, presenting him with a fait accompli. He waved his tea cup at me, in vain.

I came out of the gate just as the van went past, picking up speed fast. I took a long run at it and grabbed hold of the tailboard, almost doing myself an injury in the process. Then I hauled myself up amongst William's antique exports as he braked to turn into the main road. Safely inside I inspected the tear in the knee of my trousers ... or rather the Cambridge chemist's trousers which I'd come to think of as my own. It wasn't too bad, and I was otherwise unhurt.

Not so the corpse behind the Edwardian Screen at the back of the van. It was in a pretty bad way, awash with blood and generally very dead.

I prodded it experimentally with my little finger. It was still warm.

Nastier and still nastier, I thought, regarding it with disgust and wondering about the kiss of life. As to being Vikdor ... it was hard to tell. The face was swollen and cut about a bit ... it could certainly have passed for Vikdor. Then I had a brilliant idea and had a look in his pockets for identification. His passport provided it.

Vikdor was dead.

The van swerved and I lurched against poor dead Vikdor as we slowed to a stop.

Time to leave. So I dropped over the end and found myself in an underground garage, deserted apart from William's van. It seemed to stretch for miles, with a forest of supporting pillars which gave just the sort of cover I was looking for. I got myself to safety, four pillars away ... but only just in time.

Another vehicle came down the ramp at the far end, swerved dangerously and stopped abruptly beside William's van, the little light on its roof flashing away.

An ambulance.

The driver got out, ran round the back to open the doors, and out stepped Vikdor.

But Vikdor was dead, so it couldn't be Vikdor.

But it was Vikdor ... Vikdor a little mussed up, but otherwise much as I remembered him. He stood by watching as William and the ambulance driver unloaded the other Vikdor, the dead one, from the back of the van and carried him carefully to the ambulance. A moment later it shot away, leaving William and Vikdor standing by the van.

'Most satisfactory,' Vikdor said. 'Your driver struck me right outside the Embassy.'

'We do these things well,' William said. 'You can count on Eternity.'

They walked towards the front of the van. 'When do you expect the cargo?' Vikdor said.

'It's coming through,' William said.

'After this it had better,' Vikdor said. 'I wouldn't like to think I'd burnt my boats for nothing.'

'Here's to Bloody Mary,' William said, 'she'll make up for all your trouble.'

Then he slammed the van door and started up the engine. This time I didn't dash for it. I needed time to think things out. I had a feeling I'd just witnessed the second stage of one of Eternity's deaths, the type people came back from. It was also a little upsetting to learn that Bloody Mary was on the way after all.

I came up from the subterranean depths and found myself in sunny Belgravia. Not wishing to hang about I made my way up towards Hyde Park Corner, thinking I would get on the tube and go home, to think about my loyalties. Either I got in touch with M.2 and put Alice on the trail, or I waited for Grace to turn up and told her all. Their relations being what they were it seemed to be one thing or the other. M.2 being M.2 and Grace being Grace, she seemed the better bet, quite apart from paying better. Grace, after all, had engaged me to do the job. Grace was first.

Home to wait for Grace. I bought a paper at Hyde Park Corner and looked through to see if there was anything about Vikdor's accident, but there wasn't. Then I realised the time factor was out anyway.

It wasn't until I was actually on the platform that I saw the picture of the lady in sequins on the inside page.

GIRLTIME LONDON,' read the inscription, in bold type. 'Glamorous Girls-Girls-Girls in the nudelook of a lifetime. Now you see it all!'

The lady in sequins was Sylvia Clews who had set me up for shooting on the banks of the Cam, leaving dead Joe Keough to finish the job.

Go home and wait for Grace or go down town and investigate Sylvia. I let a train purr into the station and out again while I sat there thinking about it, nibbling some Cadbury's from a little red machine.

Toss up, I thought. Heads to go and see Sylvia, tails to go home and wait for Grace, who was bound to come looking for me eventually.

Tails it was ... but I went looking for Sylvia anyway, because I wanted to show her where she got off.

I looked on it, rightly, as a question of Honour.

Nobody puts me up for shooting and gets away with it.

I walked up and down outside Girltime closing my eyes as I passed the pictures of ladies in plastic leaves, so as not to have them interfere with my concentration. High level action stuff ought to be pure, in my opinion, having been brought up on Biggles and Dick Barton.

A large man in a gold braid uniform stood in the door of Girltime chatting to an evil looking man in a pinstripe suit. Cardboard ladies stood around them looking lascivious. I had faint ideas about loitering at the stage door and waiting for Sylvia Clews to come out when I was going to savagely set upon her. It was at about this point that I became vague. Eventually she was supposed to give a tremulous quiver and tell me all about Eternity, but the bit that was to take place in between had me worried.

I'd already been round the block, looking for a stage door, but I couldn't find one. I was standing looking in the window of the banjo shop opposite when the grey car sneaked up to the pavement and Lefle stepped out, with William Talbot at his elbow.

This was a bit of a surprise because Lefle was supposed to be in Holyhead or en route to Dublin, where the confrontation with Eternity was to take place.

They passed quickly through the club doors past the gilded doorman, but not so quickly that I was denied a glimpse of the worried expression on Lefle's face.

I strode boldly across the road, facing up to the gold

braid uniform as though I too had seen action in the desert under Monty.

'How much is membership?' I said, trying to look like a tired businessman.

'Five guineas,' he said, adding an unconscious and somewhat belated 'sir.'

'I'll think about it,' I said, knowing quite well that I wouldn't, five guineas being out of the question, I don't know how these tired businessmen manage it. So I sidestepped his cardboard ladies and made my way round the block to the building that backed onto the Girltime premises.

It had thirteen windows, all dirty. The first floor was the Candy-barque club; the floor above had crimson curtains discreetly drawn over I-know-not-what depravity and the next had a flashing sign which announced it was Irene.

I climbed the steps nervously and pushed open the door. The Candy-barque was evidently going into a decline for there was no one at its plastic bar except a decadent looking teenager in a purple and green jacket who didn't so much as lift his head from the plate on which he was resting it. I passed quickly by and up the stairs in the direction of Irene's and the unknown, which turned out to be the Merverdor Trading Company, doing a roaring line in mock Beardsley. There was plenty of mock Beardsley in evidence, but no staff, so I vaulted their little office gate and by-passed the antique typewriter to peer out through the grimy curtains at a flat roof.

It was the work of a moment to have the window up and bounce out into the open air.

'Pardon,' I said, to the Greek in the mini-pants who

was oiling himself in the shade of a green, yellow and orange awning. He smiled and said something in his own language which I took to be a remark about the weather.

'Lovely, isn't it?' I said, trying to shove up the window in the back of Girltime.

He put on his dark glasses and looked the other way, which I thought diplomatic. After all, I was none of his business. I took him for Irene's minder, and thought it was pretty tough on Irene having a casual one like that, even his minis were last year's pattern.

The window of Merverdor Trading had been a pushover, but Girltime was obviously designed to repel boarders. It wouldn't budge.

I stopped trying to force it up, and stood back, panting.

'You cannot get in?' the Greek said, sympathetically.

'I have lost my key,' I said slowly, so that he would understand.

'You may use mine,' he said slowly, so that *I* would understand.

'Thank you,' I said, 'Much obliged.'

Obviously he wasn't Irene's minder, he was one of the tired business men, and a key holder at that, with admission to the sanctums. So I went down the fire-escape and opened the little door at the bottom, then trotted back up the steps and gave him back his key, trying to convey that he was quite a decent human being for all he was Wog. Actually some of my best friends are Wogs, I just pretend I don't notice when they do Woggy things.

133

Into Girltime, looking for naked Sylvia. Flesh was the first thing that met my eyes, so I resolutely closed them.

'Pardon me, Miss,' I said, groping forward. More flesh. 'Oh dear,' I said, and darted sideways hoping for a door. More flesh. 'I'm so sorry,' I said, and opened my eyes.

Three large men were standing round me, clasping tiny towels to their midriffs. Steam was rising from the floor and writhing round them while a chubby blonde in a little blue coat stood holding a bunch of twigs and looking a bit dispirited.

'Girltime?' I said, somewhat taken aback.

'Sauna-room,' said the tired blonde. 'Take off your clothes.'

'No.' I cried, enraged.

'Come on, Ruby,' one of the men said. 'My turn.'

'Yes,' I said, 'You go on Ruby, I'll find my own way out.'

Ruby swished the fat man absently with her twigs, which were much in need of renewal. If I'd had time I'd have told them it wasn't the way a sauna is supposed to be, but I don't suppose they cared.

Down the corridor I went and through the next door, which was somebody's dressing-room. A loud-speaker on the wall gave out the Tennessee Waltz, somewhat messed about, with pauses which were all too meaningful. The poodle under the table tried to bite me, so I closed the door and went away.

No Lefle at gun-point, no naked Sylvia.

Down some stairs, and suddenly all went lush. Even the fish tank was neon lit, as was the lady with the snorkel inside.

'Is that you, Berenice?' I said, tapping the glass, because she looked like an old friend of mine from my Huddersfield days in the League of Empire Loyalists. But it wasn't Berenice. She adjusted her goggles crossly and swam off, making bubbles all the way. Berenice couldn't swim, I should have remembered, but they did look very similar in profile.

Apart from the tank, it was pretty dark down there. I hurried away from Berenice-who-wasn't, down some steps and through a door.

On the stage a lady was taking off her clothes, but it wasn't my friend Sylvia. I sat down at a table and a lady brought me a bottle of champagne.

'No thank you,' I said, firmly, having heard about those ladies. She frowned at me and picked up the champagne bottle.

'What would sir like?' she said.

'A lemonade,' I said, as the lady on the stage dropped her veil, the third one. They weren't going to get me drunk and carry me away to some cellar.

'We have no lemonade,' she said, tilting her substantial bosom in my direction, as though offering an alternative.

'In that case I'll do without,' I said.

She said I'd have to have something, it was rules. Then she brought me a glass of stout. Eternity Stout.

'Where did this come from?' I asked.

'What?' she said.

'This stout is Irish,' I said.

'Is it?' she said.

I could see she'd been carefully drilled not to give anything away. I was about to dispute the matter further when I saw Mr. Percy Smith of Eternity, the demon train driver, standing at the side of the stage with a sardonic smile on his face.

'All right,' I said.

'Six shillings,' she said.

I paid up grudgingly, keeping my eyes on Percy, who was keeping his eyes on the lady on the stage, who by now had gone beyond the bounds of decency. She wore only a tiny Union Jack where no Union Jack ought to be worn, and even that was upside down.

Eternity were in control of Girltime.

Lefle had been delivered up to Eternity.

This was, of course, exactly what had been supposed to happen, except that I was supposed to keep a close tag on Lefle and we were to bust Eternity open at the appropriate moment, when we'd got our hands on Bloody Mary.

Percy was wearing a blue evening jacket and tight trousers which did nothing for his tiny legs, though at least they were more up to date than his lush tweed suit. He didn't look like the deadly agent of an evil organisation, but it takes all sorts I suppose.

I sipped my Eternity Stout and kept myself well back in the shadows, waiting for something to happen. The only excitement was provided by a lady dressed up as a schoolgirl, who made obscene gestures with her pig-tails. I'd never thought of pig-tails in that light before, it opened up all sorts of new vistas. Of course her pig-tails weren't real, but it wasn't till she whipped them off in her finale that I recognised Sylvia Clews smiling down at her husband, Percy Smith. She threw the wig at him, and the tired businessmen laughed. She did three grinds and four bumps with an expertise which spoke of long experience, then vanished in a flash of black net stockings.

Percy had gone too.

I got up and crossed the floor quickly, out through the door marked exit, by the side of the stage. Percy was standing in the corridor, fiddling with the wig. So I hunched back against the door, drawing the velvet curtain round to cover me. In the light of the fish tank Percy unravelled the pig-tail hair and took out a slip of paper. It seemed to tell him all that he needed to know. He took a quick look at his watch and darted out through the main doors.

I took one of my rapid fire decisions and dashed after him, without so much as tipping gold braid, who didn't seem to recognise me.

I followed Percy into Shaftesbury Avenue and down to Piccadilly, his little legs going at the double. There he took a taxi, and I took the taxi behind him.

'Follow that car,' I barked, feeling very pleased with myself, because it is one of those things I've always wanted to say.

'Have you got any money?' the taxi-driver said.

'Listen,' I said, 'money doesn't come into this. I'm Secret Service. This is in the National Interest.'

'Out you get,' he said, folding his little scarf tightly round his neck.

'Well...' I said, deeply disgusted, and determined not to yield my principle, even though Percy's taxi had long disappeared from sight.

'Out you get,' he said. 'No money, no drive. They'll have me for obstruction if you hang on any longer.'

'I shall take your number,' I said, and was just warming up on the rest of a pretty devastating line I have for recalcitrant taxi-drivers when I noticed the large man coming shambling down Shaftesbury Avenue who, I divined, thought that he was creeping up on me.

It was William Talbot, and he looked ugly. Ugly in spirit that is, the sort of ugly that draws a pistol and shoots you down on the steps of Eros while you are arguing with a taxi driver.

So I clambered out of the cab and dashed through the traffic heading for the Criterion. William obviously saw that I saw, for he came belting by the London Pavilion, vaulting the railing and nipping through the cars as I bolted down Lower Regent Street and round the first turning that came to hand, making for the Haymarket. William went dashing past, on his way to Pall Mall.

I sauntered out into the Haymarket looking at the nice fried chickens across the road with pride pounding in my breast. I was half way across the crossing when I saw the second half of the killer squad, which was Joe Keough, bald head gleaming in the sun.

This time I had a good look at him. Whatever else he was, he definitely wasn't dead.

I started to run down the Haymarket and saw William Talbot coming up it, having taken a short cut. He had his gun in his hand. Glancing up the other way I found that Joe Keough was on the point of drawing his.

So I did the natural thing, which was to dive on board a passing 14 bus and throw myself in between

138

the seats as the bullet shattered the pane over **my** head.

The conductress, a nice big lady with dyed blonde hair, started to cry. A large man got up to pull the stop cord and a bullet whistled past his arm, completely unnerving him. Then we swerved into Pall Mall and stopped.

I almost knocked three nuns over as I leapt from the bus platform, pausing only to catch sight of Joe Keough and William Talbot coming steaming round the corner with their guns at the ready.

A policeman blew his whistle energetically, without inspiring much confidence in my breast. Our policemen may be wonderful, but they're not bullet-proof, and standing behind one in that misguided faith was apt to prove fatal.

He had some effect at least, for Joe Keough stopped short in his tracks.

Not so William Talbot. He saw me and came on across the road, risking his neck in a shoal of frisky buses. I watched aghast as the policeman made for him. They met on the pavement with a resounding crash which sent William Talbot's gun rolling on the ground. The next minute the policeman had him by the back of the jacket and William had given up fighting, like the old pro he was.

Wonderful, I thought, and then remembered Joe Keough.

He was standing on the other side of the Hay-market, but he had raised his gun, and was taking aim.

Not at me, at the policeman.

But it turned out that it wasn't the policeman he

was aiming at at all, because when he fired it was William Talbot who stiffened sharply, put his hands on his head and fell down.

The next minute Joe Keough was running down towards Trafalgar Square and I was running after him, from a natural desire not to be identified too closely with what had taken place. Some police forces might understand about innocent bystanders being chased down the Haymarket by men with guns, but not ours.

Our police were all too likely to ask for explanations and when those began to involve escaped prisoners I would be for the high jump. The simple thing, of course, would have been to tell all, but if I told all, I'd have the Other George to cope with, and I know what he's like. Ruthless. I'd rather face Harold himself than the Other George.

In Trafalgar Square I hid behind a lion, which seemed a reasonable enough thing to do, all things considered.

Joe Keough apparently had the same idea. He settled behind some dark glasses and three Swiss girls who were feeding the pigeons and pondering about Nelson. Policemen came and went, but there was nothing to pick either of us out from the crowd, though they did eventually fish Joe's gun out of the fountain.

Forty minutes later Joe left the square. I didn't want him to feel lonely so naturally I tagged along behind, just to see where he was going.

We wandered down Whitehall, some eighty yards between us. People were taking photographs of the guards and Danny La Rue was making a fortune dressing up as a lady, all was normal and above board in the Best of British Worlds with Big Ben echoing in the distance and Larry Olivier at the helm in the National. It was difficult to believe that the fat man in front of me had come back from the dead with such spectacular effect.

Back from the dead.

I stopped in my tracks. He couldn't come back from the dead. Therefore he had never been dead. If Small Sam the assassin and Joe Keough both worked for Eternity then his death had been quite simply a charade for my benefit. Which went to explain something which had been bothering me. Thrice I'd been at risk of death in Joe's company, once in Dublin, again on the riverbank at Cambridge, and now in the Haymarket. By rights I should have been finished off each time, but I was still alive.

I was still alive because that was exactly the way Joe Keough wanted me.

I was the one who had seen him dead. As long as I believed that, I was a walking advertisement for Eternity. But if the bullet in the backyard had been a blank all I'd really seen was Joe falling down after a bullet type bang, not quite the same thing.

He started weaving, but it seemed to be more out of habit than anything else. I didn't let it worry me, I was up to all his filthy tricks, being Southsea-weekend-trained as I've said before. I bought a paper and decreased the gap between us a little as we got across Parliament Square and down by the Abbey. We went a little way up towards Victoria and then doubled back.

I couldn't make up my mind what he was up to at

all. We were in M.2 territory, almost on the doorstep, and I had a horrible idea that he was out to bump off any of our people who happened to be passing, maybe even Alice. Past Ben we went and out onto Westminster Bridge, where he stood looking at the river boats and checking his watch.

Then the moment of decision seemed to come. He came back towards the Westminster side and I hid in the tube entrance as he passed. Back up Whitehall, and round the very corner of the building where M.2 operated.

I paused, casually inspecting a passing V.I.P. car.

He stopped, looked this way and that, and nipped through a doorway.

The doorway.

M.2 had gone over to the Wogs.

CHAPTER TWELVE

I took the underground back to Earls Court, promising myself lunch in the Yodelling Sausage to restore my resolve, but when I got there I found I was running out of funds and had to make do with a newspaper full of chips from Neptune's Kitchen. As always, Neptune's chips were excellent, but lacked that little something which lends a sense of occasion.

I skulked in Scudamore's basement, admiring their nice second-hand books though unable to afford them, but happy to be somewhere where nobody wanted to shed my blood. It made a delightful change.

The problem was whether to go charging down Downing Street to burst in on the Other George and tell him what had happened to one limb of Britain's Intelligence. I had a shrewd suspicion that the policeman at the door might not let me in and even if he did, how much did the Other George actually have to do with it? He might do something frightful like refer me to that traitor, Alice Alexander, who would promptly have me dispatched by laser beam or whatever deadly weapon she had to hand. Now I knew full well why she wasn't worried about Vikdor, she was in there with Eternity and the wicked Keoughs. The Other George was on too remote a pinnacle for my purposes, I needed aid from someone in the battle-line.

'You are interested in the after-life?' the young lady in the straw hat asked me, eyeing me through her dark glasses. I put down the old family Bible I was inspecting and smiled on her tiny person, ever ready to engage in gay repartee, even when the fate of the nation hung on a thread.

'In the right company,' I said, with a mocking smile.

'In that case,' she said, 'you must come to our meetings.'

'Delighted,' I said.

She gave me one of her pamphlets, a gay pink thing on flimsy paper and I said as I had a little time to spare did she feel like a coffee? It was only going to be a coffee too, none of your buns, because of the state of my finances.

She said that she was sorry, she had to rush, perhaps we would meet again sometime.

'Charming,' I said, congratulating myself on having shaved at the Air Terminal before buying my chips. These little things count.

'Be sure to read the advertisements,' she said, stopping half way up the stairs. 'They're the really important bit.'

'I don't understand,' I said.

But she was no more than a laugh and a thigh and a rattle of the boards overhead. So I leant against Mr. Scudamore's little steps and looked through her pamphlet. It was pretty routine stuff, A WAY OF LIFE THAT WILL CHANGE YOU, MORCHARD EVANS SPEAKS, CONSIDER THE LILIES OF THE FIELD . . . , so perhaps she wasn't my

type after all. Then I remembered the bit about looking at the advertisements. One was about acne and I
didn't bother with it having a manly complexion that
calls for no artifice, but the other brought me up with
a start, it was strictly to the point.

SWINE—WOULD YOU LIVE FOREVER? IF YOU WOULD,
BUT CANNOT, WHY NOT ENJOY THE TIME YOU HAVE
LEFT? FUN PEOPLE TOUR THE ETERNITY WAY, AND KEEP
THEIR HAPPY MEMORIES FOREVER. INTERESTED FRIEND?
RING 120-0009.

Beneath the ad. someone had scrawled in lipstick,
P.T.O.

So I turned over and read the message. 'Gerald.
Please check up on this for me. The girl is called Posy
and is engaged to a hairdresser. Book on tour P.5. I'll
see you in Ireland. Grace.'

'That will be thirty guineas please,' the lady in the
little blue uniform said to me, smiling over the
counter and displaying an excellent set of dentures.

'You will, of course, accept a cheque?' I said.

'But of course, sir,' she said.

I made out a nice neat cheque for her with a
prosperous flourish, knowing that it would lead to
unpleasantness, but feeling sure that I would be half
way round their lovely Eire trip before it came to
light. It wasn't my bank account, but I didn't stop
to worry about that. Irwin shouldn't have left his
cheque book lying about and anyway he fled the
country months ago, they couldn't touch him. It was
that or sell out my Festival of Britain Souvenirs, a
temptation which had been much before me of late,
and one I was determined to resist. My little spoons

were going to cost people pounds, someday. As it was, Grace should have thought about the thirty guineas, but she doesn't seem to think like that, not being an honest working girl.

I strode out to the waiting minibus, prepared to mingle with the fun people and find out which one of them was doing what unspeakable evil.

Four Australians, a large middle-aged lady and her husband, three Pakistanis and Lefle grinned a merry greeting to me as I clambered aboard, jauntily tilting my Eternity Tours paki-sack, the one with the For-ever symbol on the outside. I sat down beside an Australian, gritting my teeth.

Lefle didn't so much as say hello.

Which meant that he didn't want to know me. Which presumably meant that one of the others was watching him, eagle-eyed. How was I to break it to him that M.2 were in league with Eternity, that we were being led ruthlessly up the garden path?

Another lady in blue climbed on board and counted us, having borrowed the first lady's teeth for the occasion.

'Welcome to your Eternity Tour,' she said, in a nice brogue. Then she closed the door of the minibus, sat down and started up the engine.

'I didn't think they let ladies drive these things,' I said, to my neighbouring Australian, just to show I had no prejudice. After all they are in the Com-monwealth, even if they do talk funny.

'You a Brit?' he said.

I looked for another seat to move to, but there wasn't one, it being pretty poky inside. We cruised over the Hammersmith flyover and down past the ancient Doves as I told him what being a Briton was like. He had an Amazon lady friend with golden hair who listened to me with awe, as well she might.

'Wait till you see London Airport,' I said. 'That'll show you what we can do.'

'I don't think we go to London Airport,' the Australian, who was called Arthur, said.

'Gatwick then,' I said. 'Very modern. There's life in the old lion yet. Super jets and things.'

'We're going by boat,' he said.

It came as a blow. Thirty guineas and then an old British Railways boat at the end of it. Not that I'm against British Railways boats in particular, my quarrel is with boats in general and the fearful things they do to your insides, especially on the Irish Sea, which is basically nasty.

'Don't worry Jack,' he said, adding insult to injury by making an unnecessary remark about Britannia to his Amazon lady, who was on my side.

'I've got some tablets,' she said, 'if you're feeling car-sick.'

I said it wasn't the minibus, the open road had nothing on me, it was the shape of waves to come.

We stood by the rail on the Fishguard boat, the Amazon and I, for Arthur, greatly to my satisfaction, was elsewhere being sick. Around us the Irish Sea lapped gently, considering the brisk breeze which blew the rain in on us with maximum penetration. Amazon Barbie seemed impervious to it, wrapped up in her oilskins, yellow boatman type, heavens knows how she'd got them into her luggage. For my part I was still in the Cambridge chemist's suit reinforced

147

by my donkey jacket from Redcliffe Square, and not designed to resist the elements.

'Let's go inside, Barbie,' I said.

'I like a blow,' she said, golden curls cascading around her. 'You tell me more about your spies.'

It was a subject I should have kept away from, but I felt the need of a confidant, and it had somehow come out of me during the wait at Fishguard harbour. Barbie was all ears, though Arthur didn't seem interested.

'I don't think I'd better talk about that if you don't mind,' I said. 'Walls have ears.'

'There are no walls,' she pointed out.

Lefle appeared on deck, glancing furtively round him. He saw me, but he tried to look as if he hadn't, which was fair enough indication that he had, if you see what I mean. The opportunity was too good to miss, even if it did mean involving innocent Barbie.

'Don't look now,' I said, in a confidential whisper, 'but that man is in deadly danger.'

'What man?' she said.

'That man over there is pretending to be somebody else.' I said. 'I want you to take a message to him. I want him to know that the people who are supposed to think he is someone else don't, because we have been betrayed.'

'Go on,' she said, displacing all her freckles with a healthy grin. 'You tickle me, for a Brit.'

'Please,' I said, 'this is deadly serious.'

'All right,' she said, 'I'll play for the laugh.'

So I told her what to say, and she walked up the

deck, twirling her cigarette, and asked Lefle for a light. I clung to the railing and waited tensely, trying to see who was watching him, in case they tried to pick Barbie off. They talked earnestly, then Lefle turned sharply, shot a worried glance in my direction, and vanished back inside the saloon.

'Well?' I asked Barbie. 'You told him Alice had gone over to the other side?'

'Yes,' she said.

'What did he say?'

'He said,' she said, with great deliberation, 'that he didn't know anyone called Alice.'

'Cunning,' I said.

'The next time you want someone to make a fool of themselves with your practical jokes, my little Brit,' she said, with disdain, 'pick on one of your own kind. I don't find it very funny.'

'Oh,' I said.

'I'm going to look for Arthur,' she said. 'He'll settle your hash.'

I made a Pakistani move over in the coach, so that I could sit beside his friend, rather than share with my colonial cousins who were having a lot of trouble with their luggage, blue and white cases everywhere. I watched them with the lofty disdain of a veteran commuter.

'Where are we going now?' I asked my Pakistani politely, not having had time to look at the itinerary, but he didn't seem to know.

The lady with the teeth climbed in and shut the door.

'Everybody ready?' she said.

149

'Yes,' said a voice from the back seat.

I knew, without so much as looking, that Grace had somehow joined the party.

We trooped out of the minibus to look at a typical turfcutter's cottage, though there was no turf to be seen and not even a bog. This didn't deter Arthur and Barbie who were busy unpacking their cine-camera from the blue and white cases, and seemed to give me a chance to introduce myself to the small lady in the tartan trousers who stood apart from the others.

'Pleasant view, isn't it?' I remarked casually, sidling up beside her.

'Yes, lamb,' she said, without so much as a flicker to betray our present relationship.

'I do like Ireland,' I said. 'It's so back to nature. Did you know that Alice was in league with Eternity and M.2 rotten to the core?'

'The air is so refreshing,' she said, and we dawdled a little down the road. 'You're talking through your hat.'

'Joe Keough...' I said.

'Doesn't exist,' she said, propping herself up on the door of the souvenir shop, where they were selling Leprechaun logs made in Hong-Kong.

'Oh come off it' I said. 'He's been following me around.'

'Still doesn't exist,' she said. 'I've checked on the family. They come from Salop, but Joe doesn't.'

'Oh,' I said, wondering about the Cork accents.

'And the odd thing is that Maggie acknowledges him as her brother, goes to great pains to emphasise the relationship in fact. You can make what you like of that.'

'I can't make anything of it,' I said, glumly.

'I believe they're taking us to a racemeeting next,' Grace said to the Pakistani who had drawn abreast of us and was busy inspecting the old grey-haired lady who sat in front of the souvenir shop. He said that that would be lovely, and drifted into the shop with Grace, enjoying a cosy conversation.

I kicked the snow-white wall and looked down into the wooded glen, wondering where the rebels were and the folksingers and the Irish wolfhounds and the little people.

'They're taking Lefle to Eternity H.Q.,' Grace said, appearing at my elbow. 'Which means that Vikdor hasn't betrayed him yet, for reasons I don't pretend to understand unless...'

'Unless what?' I said.

'Unless Lefle has gone over to Vikdor's side.'

'Impossible,' I said. But it wasn't impossible, it was all too possible, given the sort of nasty people I was mixing with. Patriotism meant nothing to them. 'I don't know,' I said. 'People getting killed and coming walking back again ... the whole thing is crazy. I mean where does pretending they can live for ever get them?'

'You've missed the point, haven't you?' she said, somewhat irritably.

'Yes,' I said.

'It's not so much a question of swine who live forever,' she said, 'but swine who like to be thought to be dead. That's the illusion they are trying to create, not the other.'

'Oh,' I said.

She said that we were dealing with people am-
bitious enough to propose the theft of Bloody Mary,
capable enough to carry it out. They had to know the
details of the American test, they had to have their
tanker on the spot, they had to get Bloody Mary away
before they could exploit it. The men we were dealing with were obviously well versed in the organisation of espionage, with men and money at their disposal. We were looking for men whose positions
ensured that they couldn't go missing without questions being asked.

'So?' I said.

'The obvious answer is to arrange a little imper-
sonation, the better to exploit their new investment.
But the trouble with impersonators is that they're
always liable to break down. Eternity have got round
the risk. For their top brass the impersonator is a
corpse, which makes the whole thing a much easier
proposition ... especially if you pick a moonlit
antique shop to leave it in, and hinge the identification on someone who only half knows the supposed
victim.'

'So they got someone who looked like Garvey and
left him for me to find?' I said.

'It only needed a superficial resemblance,' she said.
'I'll wager you didn't look far past the ice-pick, most
people wouldn't. On the real job they would probably mess the corpse about a bit anyway, but this was
obviously a test run.'

'What sort of a test run?' I said. 'I don't get it. And
why spoil the whole thing by showing me the real
Garvey afterwards?'

'If you ask me,' Grace said, 'Vikdor asked for a practical demonstration that it could be done convincingly. The last thing he could afford would be a botched job. So they showed you the corpse, showed you to Vikdor, showed you the real Garvey, and showed you to Vikdor again, loudly proclaiming that you couldn't tell the difference.'

'Oh,' I said.

'Don't keep saying "Oh",' she said, crossly. 'Just trust me and you'll be all right.'

'I'll never trust anyone, ever again,' I said. Too many people had turned out to be something other than they were supposed to be, and always to my disadvantage. It seemed I couldn't even depend on corpses any more.

CHAPTER THIRTEEN

Being used to Ascot and Royalty with my racing, maybe I've become over-fastidious; but I could not help but look on the peeling grandstand at Kallingore with disgust, though it seemed to delight Barbie and Arthur. They spent half an hour taking pictures of each other with their shillelagh, one with a ribbon. Around them parochial Ireland let itself go in black suits and stiff collars, mucky tents provided refreshments and bookies offered prohibitive odds on favourites I'd never heard of.

It didn't seem like the place for an Eternity operation but Grace stuck firmly to her guns. Lefle was to be spirited away from our little tour, having got himself safely past the customs. It was apparently their usual mode of operation, the raison d'être for Eternity Tours.

So I paid the man on the gate with a gay smile on my lips. It was Grace's money, and she'd given me a ten pound advance on expenses, so for once I was flush, though the question of the thirty guinea cheque had still to be negotiated.

'Where now?' I said.

'Let us go and check the odds on Percy's horse,' Grace said. She hadn't told me anything about Percy Smith's having a horse before, which is typical of the way she keeps me in the dark about things.

'You didn't tell me that Percy was an owner,' I said, as we elbowed our way through the crowds. She didn't say anything, she was too busy making cryptic signals with her racecard.

'Who are you making cryptic signals to?' I asked politely.

'Don't ask unnecessary questions,' she said, a little snappily.

'Be like that,' I said, and concentrated pointedly on my racecard. After all, I was only asking. The 'Kallingore Maiden Handicap' it announced, in fuzzy type, and half way down the list of runners was Forever Angel owned by Mr. P. Smith and ridden by someone called S. Leadbetter.

'Are you going to have a bet?' I asked Grace, but she'd gone.

I may not be basically a horsy man, but I know a good'un when I see it, as I told the Pakistani who joined me at the rail as we watched them trot out. Percy being a gentleman, for all his shady connections and stripper wife, I wasn't surprised to see that Forever Angel was a very fine grey, even if the jockey did look a bit rocky. There was something about the jockey too, some faint memory that disturbed me as I made my shrewd parade round the bookmakers' stands. The average price was about tens, but I held on, waiting for a hundred to eight. You've got to have nerves of steel in this business, which is why it's like the antiques. I clutched my money and watched like a hawk. With a minute to the off I pounced.

'Five shilling win,' I barked staccato, elbowing my way through the throng. 'Forever Angel.'

Nobody took any notice. The large man on the

stand went on intoning, 'Six to one, Fiddler. Sevens Quadrille,' while the one with the big blue book beside him licked his pencil and made lightning calculations.

I tugged the large man's trouser leg. 'Nines, Rupture, Tamstime,' he said. 'Ten to one bar.'

'Here,' I said, 'down here.'

He looked down at me fiercely. 'What do you want?' he said.

'Five shilling win, Forever Angel,' I said, 'if you don't mind.'

'Right sonny,' he said. 'One dollar to ten, Forever Angel. Ticket 732.'

I didn't stir an inch. I stood there clasping ticket 732 in my hand and took a fresh grip on his trouser leg.

'Well?' he said.

'A hundred to eight.'

'You got tens,' he said, brutally.

'Five shilling win, Forever Angel, a hundred to eight,' I said. 'You had it up on your board.'

He pointed out that it wasn't on his board now. I said that that was because he'd just rubbed it out with his little white cloth. I said that it was a dirty underhand trick and I'd report him to the Bookmakers' Association or the Stewards or God, whichever he happened to believe in.

'You got tens,' he said, and went back to his business.

'I think it's disgusting,' I said in a loud voice so that all the people would hear and know him for the cur he was. Then I elbowed my way back to the rails, only to find that I'd left my Pakistani behind.

'Are you on?' Grace asked calmly.

'Yes,' I said.

'What did you get?' she said.

'A hundred to eight, Forever Angel,' I said, letting the scandalous behaviour of the bookmaker pass by default.

'That was extremely silly of you,' she said, as though I'd committed a major faux pas.

'I thought you were doing it,' I said.

Then they came sweeping down the hill, with Forever Angel well to the fore, two lengths behind a stringy chestnut who obviously wasn't going to win anything. Forever Angel looked lovely, but it was his jockey who took my attention.

'I know him,' I said, jabbing Grace fiercely with my elbow. 'That's Small Sam who kills people for the Keough's and Eternity.'

'I know that,' Grace said, as though I'd remarked on it's being spring.

I tried to look as though I thought nothing of it, but they shouldn't let a man like that up on a law abiding horse. The field swept out into the country and disappeared down a dip. 'A hundred to eight is twelve and six to one,' I said, 'so I ought to get about three pounds.' I would have been happier about it, but I didn't trust my turf accountant. They came speeding up out of the dip with Forever Angel in a clear lead.

'Come on, my Angel,' I cried, quite lifted out of myself.

'It's not going anywhere,' Grace said, in a flat voice.

'Listen,' I said. 'The breeding shows staying power,

157

which counts for a lot in a low class field.' As if to make my point Forever Angel increased his lead to a good four lengths, with the field spread out behind him, as they raced behind a distant hill. I turned round to see if the bookmaker was still there, and he was, looking quite unruffled. Even at ten to one it was fifty shillings, and my five shillings back, but I was a bit worried about the betting tax, because I didn't know whether or not they had one in the Republic.

'Do I have to pay tax on my winnings?' I asked Grace.

She said she didn't know, and it didn't matter. Then she said I'd better take a look, because they were coming round the bend into the straight. At least most of them were, but Forever Angel wasn't.

I watched aghast as a long flat chested thing with a walnut on top passed the post, followed by three others, all equally undistinguished, then came the main body of the field followed at some distance by Forever Angel, without Small Sam the killer.

'A fix,' I said, bitterly.

'I told you,' Grace said.

'You didn't,' I said, fiercely.

'Winner no. 3 Torriano,' said the announcer.

'I wonder what the odds were,' I said, wistfully.

'I got fourteen to one,' Grace said, looking very pleased with herself.

'You knew,' I said, bitterly. 'Your cryptic signals before the race. Some of your friends nobbled Small Sam Leadbetter out in the country.'

She said she'd done it for me.

'What do you mean, done it for me?' I said, filled with suspicion.

'Now you can take his place driving the Eternity van,' she said, 'can't you?'

'Oh,' I said.

She said I'd better hurry up, if I was going to swap places with him in the first-aid tent. Getting the bandages on would take long enough, let alone everything else, she said.

'Don't be silly,' I said, 'all those doctors and nurses won't let me get away with it.'

'There aren't any,' Grace said.

'It's not a proper first-aid tent if there are no doctors and nurses,' I said.

'That's right,' she said. .

I sat in the front seat of Small Sam's vehicle, which turned out to be Forever Angel's horsebox, trying to fold myself up small so they'd take me for Sam Leadbetter. Grace's nameless friends had wound bandages round my head and with a heavy overcoat I was no more than a mound in the driving seat, so long as no one engaged me in small-talk. Percy Smith being a top person and Sam very much a dogsbody this seemed a good enough bet.

We were in the courtyard of a small pub, just outside the townland of Kallingore, the rendezvous point for the Eternity Tours minibus and the official handover of Lefle to Percy Smith of Eternity and a fate which might well prove worse than death. Everybody had gone inside to drink, but as I was Small Sam the killer they had left me outside to mind the horse, which I suppose was not unreasonable, bearing in mind my reputation. There were three Eternity vans in the yard, containing the equipment from their refreshment tents and room enough for Percy and his lieutenants.

I tapped the little grille behind my head, and Grace opened it.

'How are you getting on with Forever Angel?' I asked.

She slammed the grille closed again.

I was a bit worried about the grey because of her little pink pills. After what she'd done to Imogen's birds I put nothing past her. Still, rather her than me, horses being almost as dangerous as sheep, and certainly bigger.

Arthur and Barbie, the Pakistanis, and the remaining Australians came trooping into the yard, the lady with the shining teeth shepherding them along with great tact. They all had their little tins of Eternity which meant the minibus was going to be a mini-pub on the next stage of the journey. This wasn't going to please the middle-aged couple, who had sat it out in the cold rather than enter McKenna's There were, of course, three of us missing, but the lady made only a perfunctory check. I suppose she was used to such things.

The minibus chugged out of the yard with Barbie and Arthur necking shamelessly in the back seat. I wasn't sad to see the end of them and their healthy complexions but my thoughts switched rapidly away from them when Percy Smith appeared in the door of McKenna's, clasping his bowler hat in his hand. Behind him came Lefle.

They crossed to one of the Eternity vans and

climbed in, the four other Eternity men following on, and *someone else*.

I tapped Grace's grille, and she shot it back.

'Grace,' I said. 'They've got someone with them, someone who doesn't want to come.'

'How do you know that?' she asked.

I said that I could tell by the revolver that one of the men was sticking in the back of the muffled up figure and the blanket they had put over his or her head. They loaded the unwilling one into the back of the second van, and then we all set off for the Wicklow Hills.

'Well,' I said, after we'd left the town and were riding through open countryside with high hedges on either side of the road. 'What do you make of that?'

'A routine Eternity operation,' she said, putting her cigarette through the grille for a light.

'You shouldn't smoke in there with all that straw,' I said. 'And there's no such thing as a routine Eternity operation.'

She took my point, for once, and withdrew the cigarette. 'Of course there's a routine operation,' she said. 'They want to show Lefle they mean business, a small exercise in intimidation.'

'And the poor unfortunate with the blanket on its head is a corpse to be?' I said.

'It seems a reasonable assumption.'

Down through fir trees we moved, on a road which was excellent, all things considered. We were miles from civilisation, I knew not exactly where, but we'd driven a long way.

I was getting so sleepy at the wheel that I almost

161

bumped into the Eternity van that had stopped on the road ahead of me, parked side on to the road, so that its lights shone on a rough stone wall, against which stood the blanketed figure, arms strapped tightly behind it.

They directed me on to the verge of the road, at the risk of losing Grace and Forever Angel to the plantation below, an event which seemed all too probable, as I couldn't see too well on the right hand side, because of my bandages.

'You've got the gun?' one of the Eternity lieutenants said, opening the door of my van.

'The gun?' I said, looking round for one.

'What else are you going to shoot with?' the Eternity man barked, unpleasantly. 'Come on now, Sam, wake your ideas up.'

'I don't think I can do it,' I said. 'I'm a bit shaken after the fall.'

'You'll do what you're paid to do,' he said, unpleasantly, and stalked back to the others. The only blessing was that the prevarication gave me time to find what I'd been looking for, which was the gun. Small Sam evidently believed in having his rifle to hand, it was strapped up the back of the passenger seat.

I got out of the van feeling most unhappy about it, and trying to bunch myself up small, so that nobody would notice I wasn't Sam. Luckily it was very dark and the van lights were concentrated on the miserable blanket bound figure, who was the centre of attention.

'Is this necessary?' Lefle asked, from somewhere behind me.

'We want to show you that we mean business,' Percy Smith said, his collar studs flashing. 'Take off the blanket,' he called.

Two tall Eternity men strode forward and unstrapped the blanket from the top of the huddled figure against the wall.

Maggie Keough. Her purple hair wobbled in the breeze, her make up had run all over the place.

'This woman is a small time operative for our old friend Vikdor of C.B.D.' Percy said, strolling into the patch of light from the van headlights. 'She was used to infiltrate our organisation, with her brother Joe. You may know that we got rid of Joe some time back, now it's the turn of the lady.'

I knew, and Percy Smith knew, that Joe Keough was still running round quite healthy, but he obviously intended sticking to the story which I had so faithfully told Lefle, at the time when I believed it to be true and hadn't realised the elaborate charade Joe and Small Sam had acted out for me in Joe's backyard.

'Is there any need to kill her?' Lefle asked, a little unhappily.

I could have told him I was going to miss, which made me feel very superior. Still, he'd enjoyed pulling my leg about the cherry trees when I was up against it myself, let him suffer.

'It will be a lesson to her,' Percy said, taking off his bowler and running his fingers round the rim. Then he turned to me. 'Shoot her,' he said. Thank goodness he had his mind on other things, and didn't notice that there was a lot more to me than there was supposed to be.

So I pointed my rifle a foot wide of Maggie Keough and pulled the trigger.

There was a bang, and Maggie gave a gasp, falling forward from the wall. She rolled over on her back and the bloodstain spread across the front of her jacket from the little round hole in the cloth.

I stood aghast, wondering what I'd done.

'Shall we inspect the body?' Percy said, stepping forward and butting her with his foot, but Lefle took one look at the blood and said he'd take it as read.

'In that case we'd best be on our way,' Percy said, striding back towards his van. 'Pick the corpse up and bring it along, Sam.'

The last van went purring up the hillside, leaving me with the horsebox and dead Maggie Keough, whom I'd shot down in cold blood.

I went round to the back and let Grace out. She looked much the worse for wear, with straw on the back of her suede jacket and her hair tangled, but otherwise as cool as usual.

'A terrible thing has happened,' I said, indicating the figure lying against the wall with a blanket over it. 'I have shot Maggie Keough down in cold blood.'

She looked a bit dubious. 'Are you sure?' she asked.

'Yes,' I said. 'She's all messy, and I don't like to look at it.'

'Too bad,' Grace said, as if it was a matter of indifference. 'Makes you a ruthless killer too, doesn't it?'

'I didn't mean to kill her,' I said.

'Tell that to the police.'

164

She walked over to the corpse and prodded poor Maggie with her foot.

'You see,' I said.

Then I saw something else. I saw the gun Grace was quietly stuffing inside her shirt.

'You!' I said, much taken aback. 'And you were going to let me go on thinking I'd shot her when it was you all the time.'

In the first place, Grace said, Maggie wasn't dead, just unconscious. Secondly, aiming to miss Maggie wasn't really very smart.

'Why not?' I said.

'Sam doesn't usually miss,' she said. 'He's paid not to. Your finer feelings might make you miss by a mile, but Smith would just have ordered another shot. As it was I nicked Maggie in the shoulder, she passed out, and everybody was happy.'

'Oh,' I said. Then I said she could have told me. She said I wasn't very clever with guns, or I'd have known quite well what had happened.

'I suppose Vikdor is responsible for this,' I said, as she propped Maggie up against her knee and tried to cope as best she could with the shattered shoulder.

'Maggie's in the cold,' Grace said. 'It seems like nobody wants to know her.'

'My arm,' Maggie said, in a husky voice, opening her eyes.

'You're all right,' Grace said.

'Damn them,' Maggie said.

'Let me help you,' Grace said, and helped her to her feet. It seemed diplomatic on my part to remain in the shadows. Even though I hadn't pressed the trigger that did the damage I had a shrewd suspicion

165

that Maggie might connect me with it, and Grace was unlikely to volunteer the truth.

'Come on,' Grace said, calling me forward. 'I can't get her into the box without some help.'

So I got behind and shoved, putting my hand on the back of her shoulders to get a grip.

'Isn't she heavy?' I said to Grace, who muttered something which was mercifully unintelligible. I gave another great shove and something hairy dropped onto my hands.

'Oh,' I said.

Maggie fell on to the floor of the horsebox, face up in the straw, leaving her hair behind her in my hand, every purple strand of it. Her bald head shone in the light of Grace's torch.

Grace said she thought this solved the problem of Joe Keough's being non-existent. She said I'd met them both, I should have guessed they were the same person.

It was, I said, understandable, as Maggie Keough was the first baldheaded lady transvestite I'd come across.

CHAPTER FOURTEEN

'I don't think Imogen is going to like this,' I said
to Grace as she rang the bell for the fourth time. On
the floor behind us Maggie Keough lay propped
against the wall, her wig askew, her dowdy outfit a
mess, her rest aided by one of Grace's little pills,
which do come in useful at times.

'Just speak to her nicely,' Grace said.

Imogen opened the door.

'Surprise!' I said, putting my foot in quickly.

'What do you think...' she started to say, then she
saw Grace and tried to close the door.

'Imogen, please,' I said, resisting her efforts.

Then Grace took out her little gun and pointed it
at Imogen and Imogen screamed. Grace waved it
menacingly. 'Open up,' she said. 'We don't want any
nonsense, do we Gerry?'

'Grace, I don't think that is...' I began, but she
wasn't taking any notice. She pushed her little gun
into Imogen's tummy and shoved her way in. So I
picked up Maggie as best I could and followed them
to the tiny sitting-room. Only the chattering of
Imogen's birds, evidently fully recovered from their
ordeal, disturbed the early morning air.

'You do have some ducky friends,' Imogen said to
me, hugging her dressing-gown around her and view-

ing Grace and blood bespattered Maggie with un-disguised distaste.

'Get her out of here,' Grace said, laconically.

'Listen ... who the hell is she?' Imogen demanded. 'Coming in here and throwing her weight about. Even the bloody birds aren't safe with your friends around ...'

'Nothing to do with me,' I said, quickly extricating myself from the sordid affair of Grace and the birds and hanging Imogen up in the cupboard. 'I wasn't here. I had to go to England ... business. You know the way things are with me. Grace is just a ... just a ...'

'Business acquaintance,' Grace said, grinning broadly.

'I don't believe you,' Imogen said, 'either of you.'

'Be like that ...' I said.

'What's more,' she said. 'I've sold your things. You owed me a lot of money, after all the time you've stayed here.'

'Oh,' I said, trying to imply just how low I thought she'd sunk. 'I didn't realise it was a business arrange-ment.'

'Tit for tat,' she said, smugly.

There was a long unhealthy silence. Imogen stood glowering at Grace and I stood glowering at Imogen. The only happy person was Maggie, and she was fast asleep, which probably accounted for her lunatic grin.

'Take her down to feed the horse,' Grace said to me. 'Or for a walk, or something ... now.'

'Like hell you do,' Imogen flounced, lank blonde hair flapping round her. 'I'm going back to bed.'

'The best place for you,' Grace said, unkindly.

Imogen snapped up her false eyelashes from the coffee table and strode out of the room, swishing her gown around her. I went after her to commiserate, but she slammed the door in my face, and turned the key.

'Imogen,' I cried, softly.

'You'll hear more about this in the morning...' she said, and turned up the sound on her stereogram, loud.

'If you stand shouting outside that door much longer you'll wake the house,' Grace said, frowning at me from the sitting-room door.

'This is personal,' I said, deeply affronted. Imogen was still being unreasonable and pretending she couldn't hear me. I was trying to find out whom she'd sold my things to and whether there was any possibility of getting them back. Apart from that I had a few things I wanted to say to her about abusing trust and thinking ill of people who were risking their all for humanity. There was something mean and nasty about it, I told her, getting quite het up about it, but all I got back was Beethoven's Fifth.

'And this,' Grace said, 'is important.'

Imogen was a lost cause anyway, so I gave up shouting through the door and went back into the sitting-room. Maggie Keough was lying on the sofa, apparently she was back with the living once more.

'Can she talk?' I asked.

'She can,' Maggie said, dryly, 'but she isn't going to.'

'Don't be foolish,' Grace said. 'Your number is

169

up with Eternity. That execution was meant for real.'

She said it as if she meant it and Maggie didn't contradict her, which took a weight off my mind. Maggie didn't connect me with her being shot. She thought Sam, and therefore Eternity, had done it, and obviously we weren't going to put her right. But she still didn't seem keen on talking.

'I know him,' she said, 'but I can't fit you in.'

'We met when you were being Joe,' Grace said.

'Who do you work for?'

'Let's just say he's a friend,' Grace said. 'A friend who just happened to pick you up when Eternity had left you for dead.'

'That isn't good enough,' Maggie said, shifting her position on the sofa. She didn't look at all healthy.

'Pity,' Grace said. 'Eternity have just tried to rub you out. If you're going to take that attitude I might just have to finish the job for them. Why not co-operate?'

'Co-operate?' Maggie said.

Grace left it there, smiling blandly and playing with the small gun which had so upset Imogen. We'd worked Maggie out on the run to Dublin, or at least we thought we had. She was playing Vikdor and M.2 off against each other, using her double identity as Joe to simplify her own affairs, whilst confusing everybody else. To M.2 she was Joe, to Vikdor she was Maggie. Sooner or later one of her two roles had to be discarded, which one depending on who was winning. Meanwhile she had been working her way into Eternity's Organisation ... and might, conceivably, have sold the others out to the Swine.

'What have they done with Bloody Mary?' Grace said.

'I don't know,' Maggie said.

'I don't believe you.'

'Believe what you like.'

'Vikdor has betrayed you,' Grace said. 'Eternity know all about you. Mr. Otley is from M.2 ... you must tell us.'

'I don't know who you are,' Maggie said, 'and I know too much about him,' she nodded her head in my direction. 'I have my orders.'

'From Vikdor?'

'Vikdor is dead,' Maggie said.

I told her quietly about Vikdor not being dead. Vikdor, I said, had gone over to Eternity, which accounted for their attempt to kill her. Then I told her about the ambulance. She took it all in, and she didn't like it ... hoist on her own petard, I was rather enjoying myself.

'I'll ask you again,' Grace said. 'What have they done with Bloody Mary?'

Maggie looked at the floor, undecided. Then she ran her hand across her non-existent hair, scooping the wig off. 'An Australian called Arthur Newcombe has it,' she said. 'They thought it safer to bring it back on ordinary tourist routes. He's travelled with Bloody Mary in his luggage.'

'Newcombe?' Grace said, 'Who is he?'

Maggie said she didn't know, just an ordinary Australian.

'Oh,' I said, struck with sudden horrible thought.

'What is it?' Grace said, impatiently.

Arthur on the bus, I said. Arthur and Barbie, who

171

had talked so nicely about my dangerous mission.

Somewhere in Ireland, pulled up in a lay-by where they could get their beauty sleep, was an Eternity Tours minibus with several Woggy tourists aboard, and evil Arthur with Bloody Mary in his baggage.

The question was where.

'Somebody,' Grace said, 'will just have to go and ask Eternity. It's the only way.'

'No,' I said firmly.

'My friend Jocelyn is on your bus,' I said ad libbing brilliantly at the cadaverous looking lady behind the little green desk in Dame Street. She wore a green and gold smock and large purple drop earrings which swung to and fro disconcertingly. 'I'd like to drive across and intercept him if I may ... I wonder if you can tell me where you'd expect the bus to be about now?'

'Tour number?' she asked.

'P.5.' I said.

'They'll be at Gulliane tomorrow,' she said. 'Moving on through Galway, then North to Donegal and down by the Antrim Coast. Due back in Dublin at the weekend.'

'You're too kind,' I said.

'Not at all,' she said. 'If you'd like to give me your friend's name, I'll check if he's on the bus.'

'Please don't trouble.'

'It is no trouble,' she said firmly.

'Jocelyn Armitage,' I said.

'If you'd like to wait a moment,' she said, 'I'll enquire.'

She went into the back of the office, behind a glass

partition. So I nipped round the desk, close enough to hear.

'Mr. Percy Smith,' she said to the operator. 'That query on P.5 he was expecting. I've got a man here now.'

By the time she got back to the desk, she hadn't.

I met Grace in The Bailey, where we sat admiring the clientele whilst we discussed the implications of Mr. Percy Smith expecting enquiries about the minibus and Bloody Mary.

'Suppose Maggie is doing the dirty on us,' I said. 'It may all be a wild goose chase.'

Grace pointed out that the minibus was the only goose we had ... and a goose with a nuclear egg was not to be treated lightly.

I drank my Guinness and thought about my woes.

'What do we do?' I asked.

'We go to Gulliane,' Grace said.

I demurred politely. It seemed to me that now was the time to recruit the might of M.2 to the job of retrieving Bloody Mary. She got quite stroppy about it. By Grace's standards, I was given to understand, M.2 had proved almost dangerously incompetent so far. M.2, she said, were back in the send-a-gunboat days. They would rush to Gulliane, she said, and make so much noise about it that Eternity would already be three steps ahead when M.2 got there. She said the situation called for ingenuity and finesse, not the light infantry.

'That counts me out,' I said, not altogether unhappily.

'You can hold my hand,' she said sweetly. 'You can also go back to tell the tale if anything goes wrong.'

Just the same, I said, I'd prefer to go into action mob handed.

'One of the things about mobs,' Grace said, 'is their incredible stupidity.'

'That was meant to be withering, Gerald,' Imogen said, tottering over us, cat basket in her hand. She was, as was only to be expected given the hour, tight. The bird in her basket fluttered unhappily.

'Your cat is a bird,' I said, by way of conversation.

'It's your horse I've come about,' Imogen said, settling unsteadily on the seat next to me. I take it the horse outside the flat is yours?'

'Yes and no,' I said.

'The Gardai have towed it away,' she said. 'Causing an obstruction.'

'Oh,' I said.

'They took your friend with them.'

I looked at Grace, and Grace looked grim. 'Why?' I said.

Imogen said she didn't know. Then the bird bit her through the basket lid. She reprimanded it and went on to say that she wasn't used to this sort of thing. Why couldn't we leave her out of it, she said, winding her fingers round her rosary.

'Tell us more about the policeman,' Grace said, in a voice which boded ill for all, pigeons not excluded.

'Do you know,' Imogen said with a gay laugh, 'the funny thing is that they didn't act like policemen at all.'

'Eternity,' I gasped.

'M.2,' Grace said, looking down her nose at me. 'Alice is waking up at last.'

It was, Imogen said drunkenly, almost Holy Hour. If we didn't get down to Westland Row Station quickly we wouldn't pass for bona fide travellers. We would be cut off from serious drinking for an hour. She implied that it was more than she could stand.

'Good idea,' I said, but Grace sat where she was.

'No more drinking?' I said sadly.

CHAPTER FIFTEEN

I stood in the small dark bar-parlour, rain dripping from my sou'wester hat, the feet in my Wellingtons soggy damp, despite the aid of Imogen's climbing socks, borrowed after some argument. In the yard outside Grace sat in a stolen car watching the Atlantic breakers splash on the big black rocks. Somewhere ahead of us was the minibus, and somewhere ahead of the minibus was Gulliane.

'Chilly night,' I announced cheerfully to three small black-haired locals who sat morosely crouched over the fire, but my announcement went unacknowledged. I propped myself against the counter and wrung out the sleeve of Imogen's Aran sweater. The theory of the sweater, hat and boots, was that I would merge unobtrusively with the scenery, but the scenery wore shiny black suits and Temperance badges to open their bottles with, so the exercise could not be called an unqualified success. I ordered drinks all round, beaming at them, setting the scene for the shrewd pumping which seemed called for.

Silently, the three little locals took their large whiskeys and retired to the fire. The landlord grinned sourly at me and stroked the large black cat that lived amongst the glasses.

'I'm going on through to Gulliane,' I said, artlessly. 'Seem to have missed the road.'

'You don't want to go there,' he said, glowering at me, his thick black eyebrows meeting over the bridge of his nose. I fancied that the howl of the wind outside rose a note, the little locals clustered a little tighter round their fire.

'Why?' I said.

'Couldn't say,' he said, enigmatically stroking the cat, coiled by his hairy forearm.

'Is it far?' I asked.

'Two three mile, round the bay,' he said.

'Lovely pussy,' I said, stretching out a hand to it. The lovely pussy arched its back and hissed.

'Oh well...' I said.

'You go back where you come from,' mine host said. 'You don't want to go there.'

I straightened my hat and left, to the obvious relief of the residents. Grace was sitting in the car smoking a cigarette.

'Round the bay a bit,' I said.

'Don't look now,' she said, 'but we're being watched. Somebody's standing at the upstairs window.'

'The natives are hostile,' I said.

'Or else they've been got at.'

We drove steadily uphill till the waves on the rocks beneath us were just a glimmer of distant froth, then the road wound into a small plantation, moving inland.

'We ought to go back and take a look at that pub,' Grace said. 'I have a distinct impression that its an outpost of the Eternity Empire.' We came to a crossing and followed the sign-posted direction, taking a turn that bent sharply away from the main road.

177

After fifty yards it became no more than a track. The car bounced awkwardly, and Grace killed the engine.

'Well?' I said.

'We go back and take a look at that post,' she said.

'We'll get soaked,' I said, but back we trotted. 'Gulliane 3' the signpost said. I showed great strength of character in not saying anything nasty to her, I just smiled.

'Push it,' she said.

So I pushed it, and it pointed the other way.

'Nice,' I said. 'Specially adjusted for our benefit.'

'It seems a shame not to co-operate,' Grace said. We plodded back to the car and past it. The track looked harmless enough, no ravines to crash down into or hidden machine-gun-posts.

"Well?' I said.

'Suppose we let it run down the hill on its own,' Grace said, 'just in case.'

So we did. And half way down the hill the trundling car became a roaring blasting fireball, exploding head-high amongst the bushes, shooting flames into the air, setting light to the thick undergrowth and stubbly trees around it.

'Mined,' Grace said, nonchalantly.

I sat down on a rock and then got up again, because it was all wet and not good for the Cambridge chemist's trousers, all that remained of my travelling outfit. 'What do we do now?' I said.

'We wait round for the party from the pub,' Grace said.

We were no more than a rustle in the undergrowth

when the van stopped at the crossroads. We heard the door slam and someone started down the path towards the glimmer of the burning car. Fortunately the heavy rain had stopped the fire from spreading, but we would still have been adequately fried, had we been inside. As a result we didn't look on the van people with any great affection.

At Grace's signal I moved after her down the side of the ditch towards the car, where the innocent who'd gone to make sure of us stood outlined against the smouldering wreck. It had fallen some way from the track, breaking through the undergrowth. Our quarry had got as near to it as he could and was busily engaged looking for little bits of us.

We moved in quietly on either side of him, but it was Grace who did the nasty blow behind the neck bit, for which she has a knack. He slumped over with a gasp, the torch in his hands going rattling on the path.

'Know him?' Grace said, looking at the bundle at her feet.

'Percy Smith,' I said. 'Eternity odd-job man.' Then I took the revolver from his coat and pocketed it, just in case he came round.

'No need to bother,' Grace said, 'take his coat.'

I thought she was being considerate, but she wasn't. When I had his coat on she suggested I take a little walk up to the van where I was to overpower whoever was sitting inside it. I was still arguing about it by the time she'd finished tying Percy Smith to the tree in a most methodical manner which suggested that he would be there if and when we chose to come back for him.

'You can't leave him there,' I said, 'he'll catch his death of cold.'

She said that that was the general idea. Then she said if I didn't get on with it she'd be in much the same difficulty herself.

'What are you going to do?' I said.

'I'll work round the back and give you cover,' she said.

So I started bravely up the path towards the van, feet skidding on the damp rocks, splashing in the puddles. With the van in sight I decided to take my time ... there being no dividend in being caught in the beam of a torch and summarily dispatched while Grace was still working her way in behind the enemy. I couldn't see or hear her at all, which spoke volumes for her tracking ability, but didn't help me raise steam for the final twenty yards towards the van.

'Smith?' Somebody said, and I heard the door being pulled open.

Get to grips, I thought and came quickly on.

'Is that you Smith?' the voice said.

Then the headlights clicked on, catching me clear in their beam. There was no going back so I lurched forward, half dazzled, but making for the man who sat in the driver's seat. I went in with every intention of thumping him with Percy's Smith's revolver, but he hit my hand sharply and it went west. The result was that I made do with grabbing his hair and we both went over and fell out of the van and down into the puddles beside it. With my usual fortune I ended up underneath, but a swift thrust from the Wellington boot sent him back against the front wheel. I was up on to my knees when he came back with a roundhouse swing. I ducked, and only realised he hadn't been fighting bare-fisted British when the spanner in his hand clanged against the bottom of the van. I made a grab for his spanner hand and he hit me with terrific force on the shoulder so that I went back against the side of the van. Then I saw the spanner coming again and was just about to duck when it stopped in full swing.

'Otley!' he exclaimed. I thumped him. Then I realised he was Colonel Lefle of M.2.

'I'm so sorry,' I said, and bent forward to pick him up from the puddle he'd gone back into.

'You want to watch who you're hitting,' he said sourly.

'You want to watch who you're blowing up,' I retorted bitingly.

'Get in the van,' Grace's voice said, from the shadows.

'It's all right Grace,' I said. 'It's Colonel Lefle. He's on our side.'

'He may be on your side,' Grace said grimly, 'but he isn't on mine.'

'Listen...' I said, and stepped towards her. Out of the corner of my eye I saw something flash in Lefle's hand. It was my misfortune that I turned into the path of it, for the bullet took me full in the shoulder, spinning me sideways against the van just as Grace's gun spat in reply. I went down in the puddle with my shoulder on fire as Colonel Lefle slumped backwards, hands clamped across his chest.

For the second time since my arrival in Ireland I had reason to speculate on the nature of heaven. This time there was no smell of cat to spoil the illusion, but bracing ozone was all about me and waves on the rocks stood in for the rhythm section. Overhead was a full and golden moon, and the rain had passed over. Grace stood framed in a doorway with her back to me, and I was lying on the van seats in a house with no roof.

'Hello,' I said.

'You've been a long time coming round,' she said.

'I was shot,' I said, rather splendidly, proud of myself for not mentioning that if I hadn't stepped into the path of the bullet she would have caught it.

'You were grazed,' she said. 'And we can't waste much time on it.'

I investigated my numb and bandaged arm to see if she was telling the truth. It felt pretty sore, but I could wiggle all my fingers without difficulty, and I still had fingers to wiggle, not to mention a shoulder and an elbow, which seemed to account for all the bits I'd reason to expect to be there.

'You do realise I'm in agony?' I said, sitting up.

'Later, please,' she said.

So I came to join her in the doorway. It had been a nice little cottage once upon a time, but built for four foot high people. Now what was left of it stood derelict on an outcrop of rocks, the Atlantic dark and choppy beneath it. In the distance the lights of a small pier shone out across the water, which just had to be Gulliane.

'Where is Colonel Lefle?' I asked.

'At sea,' she said, crisply.

'You don't mean . . .' I gasped.

'And his van,' she said in a bored voice. 'And before you start . . . Vikdor knew all about him. Vikdor didn't tell Eternity. There had to be a reason for that.'

'Oh,' I said. 'Are you sure?'

'I hadn't time to be sure,' Grace said. 'He was going to shoot me, remember? I call that evidence.'

'Alice won't be pleased,' I said.

On the contrary, Grace said, Alice would be delighted. Then she said if I thought about it a bit I would realise that Alice was on to Vikdor all the time, playing his game with Lefle just to keep him happy. 'If she'd wanted it to work,' Grace said, 'do you really think she would have involved you?'

Coming from a lady I'd just saved from being shot I thought that was a bit thick. 'How could Alice know that Lefle was double-crossing her?' I demanded.

Grace gave me a withering look. 'Maggie Keough is an M.2 agent,' she said. 'She's been doing the real investigation all along.'

I thought about it a bit. Then I said, 'You needn't be so smug about it, you've only just worked it out yourself.'

'Don't be silly,' she said, front teeth tight on her lip. I was very pleased with myself, because it showed her fallible like the rest of humanity. I might even have worked it out for myself . . . on the other hand, I might not have, in which case I too would have been shot dead by Colonel Lefle in the glen above Gulliane.

'You're very clever,' I said, thinking flattery might get me somewhere preferably away from the action.

183

'We'd better get going,' she said.

'Going where?' I said.

'To Gulliane,' she said.

'That would be very foolish,' I said.

'Why?'

Because, I said airily, it looked as if somebody had got there before us.

'What do you mean?'

Then I pointed out the four large dark shapes that were slipping across the bay, on their way towards the lighted pier. They were moving swiftly in on the beach, swathing white wakes behind them, a small scale invasion. 'The light infantry,' I said. 'M.2's gunboats.'

Grace swore and started across the rocks in the direction of the distant lights, but it was obviously a lost cause. Personal intervention and low cunning were out, they'd got down to bareknuckle stuff.

But it wasn't M.2 who took the initiative. The first blow was something that came screaming and screeching out of the cluster of buildings above the pier and ploughed into one of the swift running launches, lifting it out of the water and tearing it apart. Then searchlights went on, sweeping back and forth across the bay, sirens screaming and hidden guns spitting flame. The launches skimmed furiously on towards Gulliane and the fire grew heavier. Eternity had taken no half measures; Gulliane, apparently a little fishing village, was obviously little short of a fortress.

We came to the end of the rocks and were on our way to the road that wound down into the main street when the second wave of the attack came out from the woods behind us, a furious blast of small fire backed by the ominous trundling of armoured vehicles on the steep winding road.

'Get back...' Grace snapped, and back we went, down to the cover of the rocks, and only just in time, for the very next moment the road beside us disappeared in a cloud of dust and flying rock. But even before the smoke had cleared we could see the attackers moving in, firing as they ran. It was impossible to tell how many there were ... at least it was impossible for me, because I was keeping out of bullets' way, doing my best to be mistaken for dead.

'Bloody fools...' Grace said. 'They must be mad.'

Three large lumbering vehicles went past, heading for the lighted buildings. 'They can't hold out forever,' I said. 'It seems to me that M.2 are bound to win.'

'They've got one weapon that M.2 haven't,' Grace said bitterly.

'They wouldn't use that,' I said.

'They might,' she said, 'they just might, they've nothing to lose.'

Most of the attackers had gone in and the firing had faded to sporadic bursts when we left our cover and started making our way down into what was left of Gulliane. What activity there was seemed to be centred on the pier, and a large white building called the Gulliane Arms. On the way there we passed burning cars and houses and every sign of short violent resistance, including corpses, lying where they'd fallen. An uneasy still had settled on the place, and the attackers had settled in round the hotel, training

Eternity's own defensive searchlights inland on what was apparently their H.Q.

'Come on out,' someone called. 'There's no purpose in resisting further.' Even the speaker didn't seem very certain about it. If Eternity really were sitting on Bloody Mary they still had a strong hand to play.

'Mr. Otley,' a tart voice said in my ear, and I surveyed the stout figure in khaki with dismay. Alice Alexander of M.2 frowned at me severely through her steamed-up glasses. 'You are wounded?' she said.

'Yes,' I said.

'You should not be here,' she said. 'We did not expect you.'

'You put me at Lefle's mercy,' I said indignantly. 'You let me go on thinking he was on the level...'

'Somebody had to do it,' she said. 'The powers that be held that you were ... not indispensable.' She smiled a thin mean smile, and there was a moment of distinct antipathy between us.

'As far as I'm concerned,' I said, 'you can stuff M.2.' Then I turned to Grace, 'Come on Grace,' I said, 'I'm not staying here to be insulted.'

But Grace had gone.

Alice clamped her N.H. teeth in a mirthless grin. 'Your friend Grace has probably got herself shot by this time,' she said. 'Candidly it wouldn't bother us if she did. That young woman is a menace.'

'Coming from you,' I said, 'that's sick.'

Meanwhile the voice on the loudspeaker was continuing its one way conversation with the closeted leaders of M.2.

'It's only a matter of time,' Alice said, her podgy

186

face giving every indication that she knew quite well it wasn't.

There was a sudden stir as Garvey appeared at the front of the hotel, standing framed in the doorway, not in the least put out by the lights beating down upon him, or the expectant faces behind the guns. Behind him came Arthur ... clutching a blue and white suitcase.

'Bloody Mary,' I said, and Alice looked grim. She stepped quickly forward to meet him.

'Don't touch the case,' Garvey said, when we were still twenty feet away. 'If you come too near my men have instructions to fire at it ... the result could be most unfortunate, for all of us.'

'What do you want?' Alice said.

'Shall we go inside and discuss it?' Garvey said, most urbanely. 'In the circumstances I think that would mean less strain on all of us.'

Alice hesitated. 'Alone?' she said.

'My dear Miss Alexander,' Garvey said, rubbing gloved hands together, 'You really have very little alternative. But if it makes you happy you can bring Mr. Otley with you. We have plans for Mr. Otley.'

'Oh no,' I said. Alice snapped her fingers and something was prodded into my back from the crowd behind. I knew from the feel exactly what it was ... resistance was futile.

We were on the steps of the hotel and about to go inside when all the lights went out.

Grab Arthur, I thought, and lunged forward to where he'd been. I hit somebody who went over, and at that moment the guns started firing wildly all around us. Somebody tried to kick me out of the way, but I grabbed the bad foot and sent its owner sprawling. Then a torch light went on and I saw Grace, clutching Bloody Mary, bending over the still form of Arthur. She looked up, startled, and somebody fired. She leapt sideways, and the suitcase struck against the verandah steps and broke open.

It wasn't Bloody Mary. It was several dirty shirts, and Arthur's cine-camera. Then I heard the noise I should have been expecting, the whirring wings of a helicopter, from somewhere beyond the hotel.

Vikdor. Vikdor arranging his own escape, with Garvey and fake Bloody Mary providing a cover for him. We both had the same brainwave. To the right of the hotel entrance was an entry, and we reached there at the same moment ... close enough to the field beyond to distinguish the hovering craft and the figure that spun perilously on the ladder which was being drawn up inside it. He must have seen us at the same instant, for he shouted something to the helicopter pilot, and the next moment we were under fire, and forced to throw ourselves up against the wall, to take advantage of its angle.

'Your gun,' Grace said.

'Haven't got one,' I said.

'Percy Smith's,' she said. 'For God's sake hurry up with it.'

I gave it to her. She stepped out from the wall, raised it and fired. Nothing happened. Percy's gun wasn't loaded. Bullets snapped against the wall by my head as she swung the gun in an arc and threw it with all her might.

Something happened to the helicopter ... it

188

lurched violently, suddenly out of control. Then I saw the pilot was hanging half out of it, hands clawing at the rope ladder. The helicopter dipped sideways and he fell out.

'You hit him,' I said, as the pilotless machine came careering towards us. Vikdor dangling helplessly from the ladder.

'Get down!' Grace cried and the next minute the wall over our heads was falling, bringing with it the crumpled mass of the helicopter.

I was on the ground, with my head between my thighs and my arms clasped over it and things falling on me. When things stopped falling I got to my feet and staggered forward.

A man was standing holding his head in his hands. He saw me coming and lunged at me, but I got in first with a short and nasty chop which was more of a reflex reaction than anything else. He fell over and I found myself standing over him, feeling very dizzy.

'Stand where you are,' Vikdor said, looming over me. In one hand he held a luger, in the other a blue and white suitcase which just had to be Bloody Mary.

I thought about jumping him, and thought better of it. He was in a bad way, with a streak of blood across his forehead and the leg of his lightweight suit in tatters.

'You'll have to carry this,' he said, shoving the suitcase into my hand. 'But don't try anything funny.' Then he nodded at a gateway beyond the pile of burning rubble that was all that was left of the helicopter and the side of the Gulliane Arms. 'Through there,' he said.

So I went through the gateway and found myself in a cobbled yard.

In the centre of it stood a large black Rolls, and one of Alice's mercenaries, who raised his gun. 'Stop,' he said.

'Get back against the wall,' Vikdor said. But he didn't point his gun at the mercenary, he pointed it at the suitcase.

'Get back against the wall,' I said. 'He'll blow us all up if you don't.'

The mercenary looked doubtful.

'In the car,' Vikdor said, curtly nodding to me. 'You're driving, where I can keep an eye on you.'

Another gunman appeared in the gateway, followed by Alice in her khaki. Vikdor signed them back against the wall. The gunman went to raise his weapon and Alice grabbed the barrel.

'Very wise Miss Alexander,' Vikdor said, and opened the door of the Rolls. He took the case from me and loaded it inside. Through the open door he said to her, 'Mr. Otley is about to drive me to freedom. I don't want to be followed, is that understood?'

I looked at Alice and shrugged, then I turned on the engine. She signed to one of her men who ran forward and opened the yard gates for us as we trundled slowly out, turned in the courtyard before the hotel and drove slowly up the steep road out of Gulliane.

Then I took my foot off the accelerator and came to a momentous decision. I pulled into the side of the road and turned round in my seat to smile at Vikdor, sitting with Bloody Mary on the seat beside him. He

190

said something which sounded pretty foul, but I couldn't catch it. It didn't really worry me. The Eternity Rolls was constructed so that people couldn't get out of the back seat unless you wanted them to, and I didn't want him to.

'You can come down now dear,' I said to Grace, who was clinging precariously to the roof. She slipped to the ground, her clothes all mussed up, her hair badly singed. 'You made a lot of noise leaping from that courtyard wall,' I said. 'It's a damn good job he couldn't get out of the car.'

'Well done,' she said.

'And now?' I said.

'We can't do anything until we detach him from Bloody Mary.'

Then I told her about the little red button on the dashboard which I'd pressed as we drove up the hill. Eternity's Rolls, I told her, was a gassy Rolls. Behind us the monkey hissed happily, little green hat set jauntily on his head. Vikdor wouldn't do any damage to us, I said, and to prove my point he slipped forward off the seat.

The sirens of Alice's advance guard sounded on the road below us as I opened the door. On the seat above Vikdor's head lay Bloody Mary, and Vikdor's gun.

'He might still have blown us up,' I said, handling it ruefully.

'Vikdor,' Grace said, 'is not the suicidal type. Now if you'll hand over Bloody Mary I'll be on my way, before your friends arrive.'

'Leaving me to do the explaining,' I said bitterly, as she took the case.

191

'It's better that way,' she said, 'I can run faster on my own.'

I was about to carry the debate further when she pointed past me at Vikdor and said. 'There's something else on the floor behind him.'

I stepped back inside the car to investigate. I couldn't see a thing.

She slammed the door shut, ramming the window handle into my back.

'Double-crosser,' I cried.

Grace bent down by the car window, giving me the treatment with her teeth. Then she patted her jacket pocket ostentatiously.

Taking my cue, I stuck my hand in my own pocket.

Lovely money, wages of sin.

I looked up to thank her, but she was already away over the ditch with Bloody Mary.

Behind me the gas monkey hissed on, but I didn't take any notice. I was too busy counting.

C 1

Waddell, Martin
Otley Forever.